# QUEEN CITY
## OF THE
# PLAINS

The Falls of the Sioux

*A historical novel about turn-of-the-century Sioux Falls and the 'divorsays' who came in petticoats and plumes!*

# BY BARBARA OAKS
### Author of "Woman of the Prairie"

## ILLUSTRATED BY MARIAN HENJUM

*Barbara Oaks*

◀

QUEEN CITY OF THE PLAINS
by Barbara Oaks
4500 East 33rd Street
Apartment 58
Sioux Falls, S.D. 57103

First Printing 1991
All Rights Reserved

ISBN 0-9618582-2-2
Library of Congress No. 91-90347

# TABLE OF CONTENTS

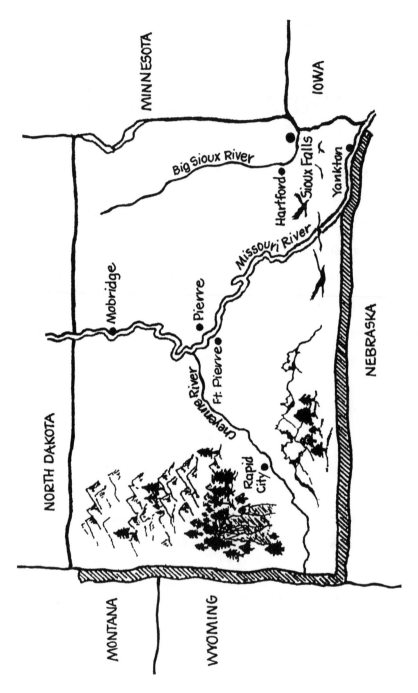

MINNESOTA

IOWA

Big Sioux River

Sioux Falls

Hartford

Yankton

Missouri River

Mobridge

Pierre

Ft. Pierre

Cheyenne River

NEBRASKA

NORTH DAKOTA

Rapid City

MONTANA

WYOMING

4

# CHAPTER ONE

# The Arrivals

The necklace was all wrong on the woman. The emeralds and diamonds which sparkled in the bright sunshine hung around the fat neck and double chin of a hefty woman in an overstuffed chair. She held herself stiffly erect, supported by the boned corset beneath her expansive dress, her legs held primly together under her voluminous skirt with just the tips of her pointed shoes protruding. She peered at the people in the large room through a lorgnette attached to a gold chain which was fastened to her ample bosom.

She was in her place in the chair she had claimed as her own in the lobby of the finely appointed Cataract Hotel. A china teacup rested on a marble topped table beside her, a sterling spoon in the saucer. A linen napkin had slipped from her large lap, unnoticed, to the floor. The daily cup of tea was her reason for being there every weekday afternoon, although everyone knew she was really there to spy on the new arrivals and report to the Bishop.

The whistle of the 3:25 train had just sounded upon its entry into the city on the east side and soon there would be an inflow of out-of-town passengers who would take up residence in the hotel for their six months' stay. Billy, the head bellhop, was at his post at the 9th Street entrance, standing at the ready in his gray uniform which gave him the appearance of a southern Civil War veteran, but which the management insisted upon as proper attire for the establishment. Several bellhops were lined up at his side, waiting to be of service and hoping for a few coins in their gloved hands. Mr. Simpson, the desk clerk, at the back of the room wore his ingratiating smile for the anticipated patrons of the Cataract, the grandest hotel on the northern plains, of which he was in charge. He checked the lobby and noticed nothing different; everything and everyone was in place as they had been for the past three

5

years and for several years before that in the old hotel which had burned to the ground. Only the faces changed periodically, with the exception of old Mrs. Goldworthy, of course.

Others seated in the room were taking tea as their afternoon diversion, napkins on their lap, the china cups carefully positioned. The men in the room would have preferred a cup of strong coffee or even a cognac and a good cigar, but there would be time for that later. They had to please the ladies in the afternoon. Now and then all eyes turned with curiosity toward the entrance.

Mr. and Mrs. Witherspoon, a small, neatly dressed elderly couple, sat on a setee against one wall sipping their tea. Mr. Witherspoon had come to the plains hoping to do research for a book he was writing on the culture and customs of the people who lived in the wild west, and he was determined to some day interview an Indian, an encounter he earnestly longed for. He was sure that an interview with a real savage, as they were called in the popular pulp magazines of the day, would be an important addition to his book. So far, he had encountered only a remarkably civilized community. Perhaps they would have to venture farther west, but the Cataract was a comfortable place at the moment. He would have to give it further thought. Mrs. Witherspoon seemed content enough. He could take his time.

Bart Kelly, a traveling salesman from the east, passing through on his way to Omaha, sat across the room in one of the many red leather chairs, close to a heavy lamp with a tassled shade. His legs were crossed and he pretended to read the paper. He sold women's ready-to-wear and specialized in corsets. He had found a gold mine in the many women of all ages who frequented the hotel and he had not continued his journey to Omaha for several weeks. He looked in appreciation over to five women who had spent various lengths of time at the hotel, who sat around a circular table under a potted palm with their tea and sugar cookies, laughing behind their handkerchiefs and whispering to one another. They had come from various backgrounds and cities east of the Mississippi and had found a closeness in a common goal. Nearby, some of the men scorned sipping tea and defied custom, smoking cigars, filling the lobby with an aromatic aroma as the smoke filtered upward through the rays of sunshine from the south entrance. Some of the women sat silently and separately, idly stirring their

6

tea with silver spoons, waiting.

Mrs. Belinda Goldworthy shifted her girth in the over-stuffed chair, took a sip from her cup, and decided it was not hot enough. She waved her jeweled hand at a waitress in a striped gray uniform. A white apron circled her waist and a ruffled cap sat atop her head. She was standing inconspicuously behind her at the entrance to the dining room at the rear of the room close by the reservation desk. She came to Mrs. Goldwworthy's side and silently poured a cup of steaming tea from an ornate silver pot, then picked up the dropped napkin and laid it on the woman's lap. Another wave of the hand dismissed the waitress and she bent her head and returned to her place by the dining room door to await the demands of the others. Mrs, Goldworthy continued to peer through her lorgnette, the better to see the objects of her attention.

All the chairs in the lobby were occupied and many of their occupants were familiar to her, having been at the hotel for several weeks. The red leather chairs and settees scattered throughout were colorful with gold studded nails outlining their smooth forms, but she preferred the over-stuffed chair because it accommodated her heavy form and, after months of sitting in it, it conformed to her body to her comfort and satisfaction. Besides, the red leather oftentimes made an unpleasant sound if one moved just so, a fact that the men didn't mind or, if they were aware of it, made the most of it. Mrs. Goldworthy never took afternoon tea at the hotel on Saturdays or Sundays, those being her days off. On Sundays she made her report to the Bishop alter services when she was invited to tea in the rectory.

It was April, 1904, a delightfully sunny day in South Dakota. She faced the entrance to the hotel on 9th Street on the south, enjoying the warm rays of sunshine coming through the door and windows. Except for the east entrance on Phillips Avenue, which provided limited sunshine in the morning, there was no better time of day to be sitting in the lobby than in the afternoon. Of course, the evening hours were pleasant when light glittering from the ornate chandeliers in the high ceiling created a sense of cozy warmth. Much of the daylight was blocked by the walls of The Sioux Falls Savings Bank which filled the southeast corner of the lobby. She suspected that the bank's employees were looking out the windows at that very moment awaiting the arrivals just as the rest of them were. The southwest corner contained a bar and she and the Bishop would have to make that their next project. It would be a mighty task for all good Christian folk, because a brewery was being erected on the hill north of town. Disgraceful!

She could hear Mr. Simpson behind her at the registration desk, fussing with the contents of the cubbyholes, arranging and rearranging the keys and messages to the reserved rooms. What a pompous little man he was, but he tolerated her presence and permitted her to sit in her chair in the lobby every afternoon and to take tea, even though she was not a paying guest of the hotel.

Mr. Simpson gave an imperceptible snort as he looked at Mrs. Goldworthy's broad back which had become a familiar sight the past several months, notwithstanding any kind of weather. He put up with her and was loftily polite simply because she did no harm, caused no scene, and added an air of eccentricity to the hotel's reputation. And a lot of good her spying would do anyway. Mr. Simpson was in his late forties, impeccably groomed to the point of looking a trifle effeminate. He had a thin, neatly trimmed mustache above a smug mouth which appeared to be rouged, but which was actually a natural consequence of his heredity. He thought it most attractive. He had a good life which provided him with a splendid salary, authority over everyone in the hotel, plus the chance to hobnob with the moneyed set. His broad tie was held in place by a stickpin with a fake stone that shone like the real thing. Striped trousers hung straight to his ankles, just touching the spats which covered polished shoes. Mrs. Goldworthy thought he looked like a waiter who fawned over wealthy diners. But he knew his job and had been at it for many years. And they both knew that he was ready for the afternoon traffic.

Mr. Simpson's eyes checked to his right where wide stairs led to the upper floors next to the fancy grillwork of the open elevator where its attendant in his gray uniform awaited passengers. A news stand stood between the elevator and the bar in the southwest corner. It contained copies of *The Daily Argus Leader* and the *Sioux Falls Journal,* assorted magazines and a few tattered brochures which had seen better days. He nodded approval of the crowded lobby. The waitress stood behind him in front of the glass doors which led to the dining room, having refilled the teacups of the occupants of the room. A quiet air of expectation could be felt, though no one could say why, because the scene had been repeated daily for a good many years.

Mrs. Goldworthy took another sip. The sound of horses' hooves clip-clopping on the stone paving was heard and soon carriages were seen through the wide doors with the largest, most imposing carriage in the lead. The bellhops straightened to attention and Billy opened the doors, smiled broadly and greeted the passengers as they emerged from their cramped quarters and passed through the doors to their new residence for the next six months plus a few weeks.

A stately woman of obvious breeding in her late thirties swept into the lobby without a glance at Billy. All eyes looked her over approvingly, taking note of her velvet traveling suit, the high necked lace blouse and a wide brimmed hat tied beneath her proud chin with a chiffon bow. She was a handsome woman dressed in lavender and trailing an expensive scent to an appreciative Billy. She was followed by two young women, servants from their dress and demeanor. They carried large valises in each hand and refused Billy's offer of help, informing him there were more bags and a trunk in the dray behind the carriages. Billy gave the order to two assistants to bring them in and turned to the next arrival. He directed another to help a short, stubby woman who was puffing and perspiring from the exertion of her journey and the difficulty of transporting her luggage. Her brown suit dress was rumpled and worn and her plain brown hat was askew on her head, but her plump face bore no trace of irritation, just patience with a touch of resolve. She was followed by a handsome couple who were dressed far differently from anyone who had ever arrived at the hotel. He was tall and slim, dressed in a casual ivory linen suit with matching broad brimmed hat and he carried a fancy walking stick. She was attired in a long soft skirt of pale pink gathered at the waist with a dark rose satin belt. A fringed shawl hung over her small shoulders and her long blond hair, which hung almost to her waist, was tied back with a matching rose satin bow. They moved lazily into the lobby, looked about with feigned disinterest, but took in their surroundings with concealed surprise at finding such a civilized atmosphere in South Dakota. They were young, from wealthy families as was apparent to all who stared at them, and they were attached to one another judging by the way they clung, moving and acting almost as one. Mrs. Goldworthy's eyes widened and she

9

dug into her beaded purse for her tablet and pencil to make a note as the bellhops fetched the couple's expensive luggage from the dray. There were two more entrants, a man and a woman, traveling separately and independently, who looked tired. She was of average height, pleasant appearing and neatly dressed in a blue traveling suit and small hat. He was good looking, dark complexioned, and dressed in a dark suit and bow tie, with a fedora covering his short hair.

"Good day, Mrs. Clayborne," said Mr. Simpson to the grand lady who had led the procession to the desk. "Welcome to the Cataract. I trust your trip was pleasant."

He handed the haughty woman a quill pen and moved the registration book toward her. Mrs. Clayborne signed with a broad scrawl, accepted a key from Mr. Simpson without so much as looking at him, and turned to the elevator, followed by her two maid servants and two bellhops loaded with the rest of her luggage. Imperiously, she directed the elevator boy to take them to a suite on the fifth floor. The doors closed on the crowded group that was crammed into the slow moving elevator, as well as on the frozen smiles on the faces of the uniformed bellhops who were sure of a large tip and thankful for the good fortune that had directed the fragrantly perfumed, elegantly dressed Mrs. Clayborne to them.

Mr. Simpson handed the pen to the short woman who had been grateful to catch her breath while Mrs. Clayborne's party was being taken care of. She had paid little attention to them, but had looked around the lobby with interest. She signed the register with an effort, as the desk rose imposingly before her and she could have used something to stand on. She took her key and smiled back at Mr. Simpson as he said, "Thank you, Madame Culpepper." She walked to the elevator and waited for its descent, which she assumed would take awhile, and watched as the young couple who had followed her into the lobby registered. They looked so in love, like newlyweds.

They were not newlyweds. Mr. Simpson talked directly to the young man, not missing a thing in his appearance, a bit envious of him and how the finely tailored linens hung on him, the casual way he wore the silk scarf at his young neck, and his Italian shoes. He had not bothered to remove his broad brimmed hat. Mr. Simpson's touch of envy was swept away by this breach of etiquette.

"Yes sir, Mr. McCallum. Your rooms are ready. Adjoining

rooms with bath on the fourth floor. The boy will see to your bags."

A snap of his fingers brought a bellboy to attention and he led the way to the elevator where they joined Madame Culpepper, who smiled amiably at the young couple. The young woman returned her smile. The elevator doors opened and they got on, sorry to miss the registration of the remaining man and woman. Mrs. Goldworthy was writing swiftly in her tablet at the scandalous news — adjoining rooms indeed!

"Ah yes, Mrs. Anderson," Mr. Simpson was saying. "I have your room ready, one of our more modest accommodations," he said with condescending courtesy. "If everything is not to your satisfaction, just let me know and it will be corrected at once." He handed her a key and she picked up her suitcase, glad not to have to pay a bellhop, since they were all occupied, except for the young man who was still at the entrance. She wearily took her stand before the elevator.

"Mr. O'Toole, isn't it?" continued Mr. Simpson. "All is in readiness for you. I hope you enjoy your stay. The Cataract has everything you will need, food, service, entertainment." Mr. O'Toole accepted his key and waited in silence at the elevator with Mrs. Anderson. Neither glanced at the other. The elevator returned to the lobby at last with its smiling operator. Mr. O'Toole motioned for Mrs. Anderson to enter and followed her with his black suitcase.

The onlookers in the lobby put down their cups in unison, The show was over. Bart Kelly got up and left the hotel to get some cigars. The women at the round table under the potted palm left to do some shopping. Mr. and Mrs. Witherspoon went upstairs via the steps to have a nap before the evening meal. They always took the stairs because Mrs. Witherspoon claimed it was good exercise for them, after which Mr. Witherspoon was grateful to lie down. Mrs. Goldworthy put her tablet and pencil back into her beaded purse, hoisted herself from her comfortable chair as the napkin slipped to the floor, adjusted her roomy skirt, heaved a satisfied sigh, and moved toward the door. Billy politely opened it with a slightly exaggerated bow as the old woman made her exit. No tip for him today, but tomorrow would bring new opportunities.

# CHAPTER TWO

# The Queen City

Sioux Falls lay in the southeastern corner of the State of South Dakota. The Big Sioux River, which branched north from the Missouri, circled the city and tumbled over the Falls of the Sioux on the outskirts to the northeast.

Sioux Falls was called the Queen City, being touted as such by an 1890s pamphlet sent to the East by the thousands to hoped for settlers. The pamphlet was proclaimed "a handsome new book," measured 10 x 12 inches and consisted of 32 pages. The Reverend J. H. Mooers wrote the book which spoke glowingly of "Sioux Falls, the Queen City of South Dakota." *The Daily Argus Leader* described it as:

> " * * * having put in an exceedingly telling and attractive way a description of the natural advantages, the trade connections, and the rustling qualities which have built up Sioux Falls. * * * written for spreading the gospel of Sioux Falls through the East. * * * The book should be scattered over the East by the thousands. * * * one real estate man sold $8000 worth of property through the books already."

Each book cost 25¢ and took a 2¢ stamp to mail and brought millions of dollars into the area. The effort to entice settlers worked and there was a great demand for the book by eastern businessmen and land speculators. Investors came and were mightily impressed with the opportunities presented to them. Land sold for $5.00 to $12.00 an acre. Word sped back to the East. One Maine investor was quoted as saying "I confidently believe from what experience teaches me that Sioux Falls is certainly destined to be the Minneapolis and St. Paul of this century, if not its Chicago."

Sioux Falls was South Dakota's principal center of business, banking and transportation. In 1904 the population had burgeoned to 10,000. It was connected by railway systems from all across the nation. All lines had several arrivals and departures daily, bringing people from the crowded East who were eager to make a new start toward a prosperous future in a new land, as promised by the persuasive words they had read and heard.

The city was laid out in straight lines with avenues running north and south and streets running east and west. The juncture of 9th Street and Phillips Avenue, named after a Dr. Josiah L. Phillips from Maine, was the center of the downtown area, and the numbering of buildings in all directions began at that point, creating some confusion from its inception and for some decades to come, but which residents eventually simply accepted and adapted to. This downtown core bustled and moved with its newly found growth and its additional residents. Impressive new buildings of brick and stone sprang up, rising three and four stories and higher, all the way from the Big Sioux River on the east to Minnesota Avenue on the west, and from 6th Street on the north to 12th Street on the south. Quartzite, or granite as it was called, or as some would say, jasper stone, was found in abundance in East Sioux Falls, and sturdy buildings were erected and faced with the attractive pink rock, including the post office, the Minnehaha County Courthouse, the Carnegie Library, and the South Dakota State Penitentiary, which sat on a hill north of town. The quarries in East Sioux Falls provided employment for many workers, many of English and Scandinavian descent, who came to work hard and make a good living in the promised land of the Dakotas. But no one could foresee the deadly "stone cutter's consumption" which eventually affected them all and which caused the debilitation and deaths of most of them.

In the forefront of the development of Sioux Falls was a local entrepreneur, Richard F. Pettigrew, largely through whose efforts the city was founded and prospered. He developed the first transit system and made a noble effort to harness the power of the Sioux, resulting in the building of the Queen Bee Mill which towered seven stories above the granite which surrounded the falls. A distance to the south the Cascade Milling Company building stood, its purpose being to produce flour. Pettigrew needed a wealthy investor and conducted a search in the East, notably New York, for someone to finance the construction of the two edifices. He convinced a George Seney, an investment capitalist, to come to Dakota and check out the site. Before his arrival in June, 1879, Pettigrew had a temporary earthen dam built across the Big Sioux River north of Sioux Falls. Immediately before Seney's arrival the dam was removed and the pent-up water roared over the rocks, greatly impressing Seney and giving impetus to his investment. However, the Queen Bee Mill and Cascade Milling Company failed and by 1900 the buildings stood tall and vacant, a bankrupt investment.

But Richard F. Pettigrew continued to boost the qualities of the City of Sioux Falls throughout his lifetime, constantly promoting both the city and himself. He became the first U. S. Senator from the State of South Dakota, after a part of Dakota Territory was made into the States of North and South Dakota in 1889. He proved to be somewhat of a maverick, causing dissension in the Republican Party. As a politician he saw immense power within his grasp. His ambition knew no bounds, but the benefits he brought to the state and the City of Sioux Falls shielded him from the controversy that soon surrounded him and his activities. Upon running for another term in the Senate, the Republicans felt so strongly about the criticism heaped upon the party that President Theodore Roosevelt was persuaded to come to South Dakota to campaign against him, whereupon Senator Pettigrew was defeated. He turned to the Democratic party, then to the Populist Party, and was eventually accused of being a Socialist, but the ultimate defeat came about some years into the future, in 1917, when he was indicted by the U. S. Senate for his opposition to the entry of the United States into the first World War. However, his immense investment of his own resources of money, land and buildings was vital to the growth of the city and instrumental in putting Sioux Falls on the map.

The power of the beautiful falls was never permanently realized; however, that very beauty was a drawing power for the city. Photographs of the falls cascading over the granite emblazoned post cards and were included in magazines and newspaper articles, which helped make the city grow with its new residents from other states.

As settlers moved into the state the original townsite of the 1800s proved to be inadequate. Most of the wood structures had burned to the ground. The new city of the 20th Century was rebuilt stone by stone into the thriving metropolis it became in 1904. It boasted a half dozen or so banks, one of which was situated in the Cataract Hotel. There were as many railway lines into the city. Besides the Cataract there were other hotels, among which were the Merchant, which had a gaming room; the Teton; the Phillips House close to the Illinois Central Railroad for the convenience of less affluent travelers: and there was a Star Rooming House. Most of the accommodations were on Phillips Avenue, the main thoroughfare.

Entrepreneurs and hustlers saw the gold mine in the swarms of people coming in and, in addition to selling cheap land and providing employment for the scores of laborers who built and rebuilt its buildings, there was another, more sinister reason for the influx of people, and that was an easy divorce. From 1890 and for almost two decades lawyers, who eventually numbered more than 100, were kept happily solvent providing services for troubled men and women who wanted out of their marriages. In 1890 a three months' stay was all that was needed to establish residency in the State of South Dakota, after which a divorce could be obtained in a short time in closed court, providing privacy to those who wished to keep their divorces comparatively out of the limelight.

The proliferation of those seeking a divorce and those who helped them obtain one grew to such enormous proportions that the State Legislature changed the residency statute to six months. It did little to stem the flow of divorce seekers, because it was still half the time it took in the East. Hotels were kept busy and filled to capacity. Large homes were turned into boarding houses. And gossip in the city was spicy because of the kinds of people who filled the town, people who were like none they had ever seen. Businesses flourished from the added population. Shops and restaurants thrived.

People of note and influence came and went through the divorce mill, some of whom left their marks.

In 1888 the niece of John Jacob Astor by the name of Margaret Laura DeSteurs received a divorce from her husband, Alphonse Eugene Lambert DeSteurs, who was the Minister to the Kingdom of the Netherlands in Paris, France. John Jacob Astor was so pleased when she got rid of her philandering husband that he donated money for the establishment of the Episcopal Church, which was then called St. Augusta, in memory of his wife, who had devoted time to working with Indians. Alfred I. DuPont of Delaware was so impressed with Sioux Falls and of its treatment of him that he also donated a large sum of money for the Episcopal Church, which became a guiding force in the community.

A Freddy Gebhardt, an ardent admirer of English acting beauty Lily Langtry, divorced his wife in Sioux Falls, telling one and all that he was going to marry the Jersey Lily, who then was a very special friend of the Prince of Wales, Edward VII. However, she refused Freddy and married a Lord instead.

An actress, Mrs. Roland B. Molineaux from France, of the DuPont family, obtained a divorce from a general who had served in the Civil War and promptly married her lawyer.

Even a circus clown from Barnum & Bailey's Circus divorced his wife when the circus played the City of Sioux Falls in the 1890s, accusing her of "surrendering to the amorous advances of the circus manager."

Herbert C. Woolworth, five and dime magnate, divorced his wife in 1904, charging desertion and unfaithfulness. While in Sioux Falls he established a dime store, making it his national headquarters.

The "divorsays" as they were called, were not without certain wiles. Mrs. William Rhinelander Stewart won an annulment from her husband for unfaithfulness and made plans at once to take as her next husband a multimillionaire by the name of "silent" Smith, who was not an easy catch. They married immediately, but the marriage lasted only long enough for her to bear a daughter, Anita Stewart, enabling the former Mrs. Smith to elicit a dowery for their daughter when she married the pretender to the throne of Portugal.

The tongues never stopped wagging.

Grounds for divorce were as diverse as those seeking one: adultery; habitual drunkenness; impotency; conviction of a felony; cruelty; inhuman treatment; incompatibility; wilful neglect and desertion. Lawyers, depending upon their experience and proficiency, charged from $500 to $8000 for a divorce and were paid without a whimper. Most of the better lawyers had their offices in the Edmison-Jameson Building across the street south of the Cataract Hotel on 9th Street for convenience. All six floors were occupied and the windows lined with observers for the daily arrivals of possible clients every day. Some of the more influential had managed to obtain permission to place their cards in every room of the Cataract, an arrangement Mr. Simpson made possible for a small remuneration.

The multitude of lawyers was not without the possibility of being duped, possibly by a capricious woman, more probably by a sly bartender. In the late 1890s a wealthy woman who took up residence in the Cataract, supposedly gave out the information that she would interview lawyers in the evening at 7:00 o'clock in Room 36 to select one to handle her divorce. The lobby was filled precisely on time with lawyers, some of whom had brought their secretaries, who waited for word of their turn to present their credentials. The wait grew inordinately long and they were informed of a slight delay. Some lawyers waited in the bar, leaving their secretaries sitting in the lobby fretting at the long evening after a very long day. At last one of the lawyers went up to Room 36 himself to inquire. He soon returned with the information that there was no one there and there would be no interview, that they had been had. Disgusted, the assemblage left the hotel, but one lawyer who remained until closing overheard a bartender remark to another, "That interview story of yours was the best idea for business we've had in a long time." It turned out to be the last business from lawyers for a long time, as they took their business elsewhere to show their displeasure.

The Cataract Hotel was by far the largest and fanciest hotel in the city; in fact, in the State of South Dakota, and some would say in the entire upper plains. One would have to go to Omaha to find any better. The Cataract was situated on the corner of 9th Street and Phillips Avenue. It was brand new in 1901 when it had been rebuilt alter a disastrous fire. It took up half a square block with entrances on both 9th Street and Phillips Avenue. The facade was of ornamental brick, buff in color and it stood five stories high. It had 160 rooms, 40 with bath, renting for $1.50 a night. All rooms were handsomely furnished, heated by steam and brightened with electricity from its own plant. It employed 82 efficient workers, strictly trained, whose function was to serve its many paying guests. To be employed at the Cataract was the highest one could go in the service sector. There was a large dining room which seated 150 at roomy tables covered with white linen cloths and attended by courteous waitresses in striped gray dresses, white aprons, and small white ruffled caps. Ornate rose colored paper covered the walls, and light from tall windows bordered with stained glass gave the room a warm glow. Light from large chandeliers brightened the room for the evening meal. The cuisine was legendary with full menus for every meal, ranging from smoked oysters to fresh asparagus, with assorted meats in-

17

cluding pheasant. Wealthy out-of-town guests, used to such surroundings, were surprised at first to find such opulence in South Dakota, but adjusted rapidly and soon accepted it as a matter of course. Occasionally, local folk would splurge and take a meal in the dining room in the hopes of seeing someone famous or, at the very least, eccentric.

After the first decade of 1890 to 1900 and when the turn of the century had not abated the unsavory image of the "divorce colony," the upstanding citizens of Sioux Falls who considered the main business of their fair city to be other than providing divorces for the rich and famous from other states as a matter of convenience, became aroused enough to express their righteous indignation and concern for the future of the city. Most of the "divorcees" were women, but there were men who came, as well, and they were no better in the eyes of the citizens. Divorce was considered unChristian, not at all the thing to do no matter what, and here in residence were all the undesirables, purportedly people of note who had considerable influence in the East, who were making a mockery out of the home of the people of South Dakota. Too much unfavorable notoriety was cast on the City of Sioux Falls and something had to be done.

The religious regarded the divorcees as "social lepers and social filthiness" and worked hard to change the residency law to longer than six months' time to put a stop to the immorality. The Bishop led the fight and said, "After the new law goes into effect, we'll have no more dumping here." Many concurred with him but not everyone, especially those who made a good living from increased business. Prosperity was a distinct boon to the city and those affected by it wanted to make as much money as possible before things changed and it looked like things would remain the same for a long time.

The town was divided. All of which meant little or nothing to those who came to the city for an easy, though costly, divorce and they kept on coming.

18

# CHAPTER THREE

# Suppertime at the Cataract

On the evening of the recent arrivals the new residents of the hotel joined those already assembled in the spacious dining room. Extending from the ceiling at intervals were light fixtures which illuminated the room through tulip-shaped shades. But it was not so brightly lit as to lose the intimacy afforded those who wished to avoid the stares of strangers. The sound of the rapid footsteps of waitresses on the hardwood floors and a hum of conversation filled the air.

The dining room was filled almost to capacity when the elegant Mrs. Clayborne entered, causing conversation to become muted. Her perfectly coiffed chestnut colored hair above her fine features and her green satin gown which outlined her figure contrasted with the grim look on her face. She was followed by her two maid servants. They were led to a table in one corner by the maitre d'; it was a secluded spot away from the windows, where light from the arc lamps outside glowed softly through the stained glass outlines. She was seated with a flourish which she chose to ignore, and accepted a menu. Her maids sat across from her with their backs to the other diners while they tended to their mistress's every need.

The young, well-dressed couple, Mr. McCallum and his lady friend, were seated before one of the windows. Their reflections were softly outlined and they were completely engrossed in one another, only occasionally glancing casually around the room, making comments behind their linen napkins.

Mr. and Mrs. Witherspoon, the elderly couple, sat at what must have been their customary table in the middle of the room, slowly eating their evening meal, speaking little, and watching everyone, which constituted their regular entertainment. They were in no hurry, as once they left the dining room they would have to return to the stillness of their suite with nothing to

Mr. and Mrs. Witherspoon

do except listen to the clock tick or read *The Saturday Evening Post* until they grew sleepy. Mr. Witherspoon hankered to spend time in the bar with some of the other men afterwards, but it would never do. The resulting displeasure from Mrs. Witherspoon would not be worth it. They often compromised, with Mrs. Witherspoon's permitting an after dinner cognac and a cigar at their table, which he managed to prolong as long as possible.

The five women who had occupied a corner of the lobby that afternoon were seated together, dressed in some new finery purchased just that afternoon and comparing notes on how grand they looked; and they were looking over the new arrivals with much interest. There were never as many men at the hotel as there were women, so their attentions were focused on the new ones, Mr. McCallum with his distinctly eastern attire and Mr. O'Toole who appeared to be alone, but neither of the men paid any attention to them. Bart Kelly, the traveling salesman, stopped at Mr. O'Toole's table, ignoring the frown of the maitre d', and inquired if he would mind if he joined him as the room was a bit crowded that night. Mr. O'Toole nodded assent and they exchanged introductions. They were soon engaged in masculine conversation.

Mr. McCallum and his lovely companion dawdled over their meal, picking at the fine cuisine in front of them, moving the pieces of grilled bluefish around on the china plates, enjoying the glasses of claret which Mr. McCallum refilled from a crystal decanter. Now and then he would caress her outstretched hand, oblivious to the looks from some of the nearby diners.

Mrs. Clayborne's cultured voice could be heard placing an order for herself and her maids, declaring to the patient waitress that since she was somewhat fatigued and not very hungry she would have the consomme and the shrimp in aspic, and where on earth did the shrimp come from in this Godforsaken place? And was it safe to consume seafood in April? Her maids would have the lamb and browned potatoes she decided, without comsulting them.

Mrs. Culpepper and Mrs. Anderson shared a table. They were tired but, nonetheless, hungry and ordered the roast prime beef, mashed potatoes and French peas with some anticipation. Mrs. Culpepper chuckled after the waitress left and wondered what the difference was between French peas and American peas, causing Mrs. Anderson to smile, much to kindly Mrs.

Culpepper's satisfaction.

Mr. and Mrs. Witherspoon enjoyed the specialty of the day, whatever it turned out to be, and they were seldom disappointed as the daily change was always good. They had long ago given up trying to figure out how any hotel could manage that feat and sat back and enjoyed it, until their weekly bill arrived, when Mr. Witherspoon complained mildly to Mrs. Witherspoon about the cost, knowing he should do so, and also knowing that she would pooh-pooh his complaints as being of no consequence. She would then also say what better way to use their money — her money actually, because it was an inheritance and there was plenty of it — than to have a nice time spending it. Besides, she would add, wasn't he able to pursue his goal of writing a book or some silly thing that she was financing? And he really should get on with it. Whereupon Mr. Witherspoon would reply that he was considering the idea of talking to a real live Indian, if he could locate one, and maybe they should move on. She would promise to think about it, they would read the paper or a magazine and then retire for the night.

Mr. Kelly was regaling Mr. O'Toole with stories of the selling game, in particular that regarding women's undergarments and the hot selling corsets he promoted, and Mr, O'Toole let him ramble on, realizing that his dinner companion would talk on and on and that he would not have to offer much by way of reciprocation. Once in awhile he would ask a question about the city and what it had to offer. Both men were of Irish extraction, which was the only thing they had in common, and there was little else to suggest any sort of lasting friendship. Mr. O'Toole would make a point of avoiding the verbose Mr. Kelly in the future. He half listened as Mr. Kelly continued, offering to show him the lively spots and where to go to have a good time, said with a wink. Mr. O'Toole did not reply, but continued to savor his steak and coffee.

Meanwhile, Billy and the other help whose shifts for the day were over were welcoming the end of another day of catering to the sometimes frivolous requests of the paying guests and were enjoying the one meal allowed them before they left for their respective lodgings. There were two dozen of them seated at a long table at one end of the huge kitchen, away from the swinging doors that led to the main dining room. conversation with their own kind was a welcome relief after the forced courtesy and fixed smiles lavished on the residents of the hotel. Bellhops had removed their jackets for comfort and to not stain them with food. Maids kept their aprons on as they ate, because after their meal they were to be deposited in the laundry chute every day anyway. All of them were hungry and, though they were not served with the flair afforded the diners in the main room, they had their pick of some pretty first-rate food even though it was not considered good enough to leave the kitchen. There were no complaints and they relished their meal and each other after a hard day.

Billy sat beside Louisa as was his custom. They had begun their service at the Cataract Hotel when it was new in 1901 and had taken a liking to each other at once. That liking grew to love. They came to know one another better than some engaged couples: in fact, better than some married couples, due to their long courtship. They would be married as soon as they had saved enough money to buy a home of their own and start a family and, with the divorce mill running full force, it should not take much longer. They enjoyed their suppers together whenever they had the same shift and, in addition to murmured words of love, exchanged gossip and juicy news they had heard during the course of their duties.

Billy stuffed one last morsel of dinner roll into his mouth and leaned back, satisfied and rested. He looked lovingly at Louisa and indulged in his usual imaginings with her as his wife, having just served him his meal, poured his coffee, and taken off his shoes and socks to rub his aching feet, granting him every husbandly desire, and then permitting him to make passionate love to her. What a sweet life they would have. She was pretty, with a face made more comely with the animation she exhibited while she regaled him with the latest news. Her dark hair was curled impishly around her face and her brown eyes sparkled. In making a point she bobbed her head up and down, causing her ruffled cap to slip a bit, making her look utterly charming. How he loved her!

Louisa was head over heels in love with Billy, too, and thought him to be the nicest boy she had ever known. He had matured into a handsome man in the last three years and she was totally mad about him, would do anything for him. Her heart always turned over at the end of the day when he was all rumpled and warm and his light brown hair was tousled about his teasing blue eyes as he looked over every inch of her. She admired his build and his strength which had increased from handling the many heavy bags and trunks. Some day she would be his wife. She had always worked hard, more so in the past three years than at any other time in her young life. She had come to realize that if she had to work that hard she would much prefer to do it in her own home and for her own family, with Billy coming home to her every night, eager and waiting for her loving. It shouldn't be much longer and they would be man and wife.

They lingered over their coffee, visiting with the others at the table and ignoring the chef' s urging to finish and move on, that their dishes were needed for the main room. All of them contributed tidbits of information about any new arrivals, but were careful to not be overheard by any of the kitchen help who might report it to the management, but they were usually far too busy to pay any attention to them. Louisa was among the maids who had duties on the fifth floor that week, and the arrival of Mrs. Clayborne and her personal maids had her bubbling over with news to relate. She addressed herself to Billy, fully aware that the others were listening as best they could.

"Billy, I've seen some pretty fancy ladies in my time and anyone who can afford a fifth floor suite has to have lots of money, and you know how strange some of those fancy ladies can be. Well," she said with emphasis, "you would not believe your eyes. Mrs. Clayborne is mighty strange. Those maids of hers do everything for her and I mean everything. She doesn't lift a finger. I feel sorry for those two girls. They carried up those two heavy valises while she hung on to that shiny purse of hers with both hands, her nose in the air. And they had to tip Hank and Mike from a special black box she handed to one of them. The maid took out two coins and gave each of those boys precisely 25¢ — 25¢! And after all the work they did for her, hauling all that luggage into the bedrooms, opening that heavy steamer trunk and moving the furniture in the room around to suit her. Can you beat it? The maid couldn't look them in the eyes she was so ashamed."

Hank and Mike nodded their heads, their mouths held in a straight line. They had hoped for a dandy tip from such a lady. Louisa went on.

"But what could the poor girl do? She must have had her orders. That box rattled with a bunch of coins, too. I was emptying all those valises and hanging up some of her things, those she would let me touch, what with those girls of hers doing her every bidding, arranging her toilet articles just so on the dresser, but not before she made them dust it off. Just think of it! That dresser didn't need any dusting. Our rooms are always spotless, you know that, Billy, especially the ones on the fifth floor."

Louisa was becoming heated in her indignation and the others at the table paid close attention to what she said.

"And you should see the silver mirror with matching comb and brush she has and the beautiful silver topped containers for her hair swatches and face powder oh and it smells so expensive, to say nothing of all those perfume bottles. They must have cost a fortune. But, there is a locked diary, too, that she put in a drawer right away. Then–oh Billy, you just will not believe this part." She began to giggle. "Those two girls undressed her and got her ready for her bath. They poured this wonderfully fragrant oil into the running water and the bathroom smelled so nice. She was in there long enough for me to finish the unpacking and to store the bags and shut that steamer trunk. Then the door opened and this sweet smelling steam rolled out into the bedroom and–I tried not to look, really I did, but just couldn't help sneaking a peek through the dresser mirror–Mrs. Clayborne stood up and stepped out of the tub and those girls held up a towel for her. Then they proceeded to dry her off. I mean really–how helpless can she be? I thought I'd seen everything, but then," and she bent closer to Billy and kept her voice low so the others had to strain to hear her, "they powdered her all over and then they pulled this corset around her, hooked it up to where her waist was so small there couldn't possibly be any room for supper, and she stepped into some sheer silk stockings as those girls pulled them up, one on each side of her, and hooked those stockings to her garters." Louisa's giggle threatened to get out of hand, and she wiped her eyes. "Can't you just see it?"

Billy could quite imagine. There was a buzz of conversation at this choice piece of gossip. Billy looked at Louisa. They finished their coffee and left the kitchen by the back door. He would walk her home and get his goodnight kiss.

# CHAPTER FOUR

# The Runaway

Gretchen Nielsen finished the breakfast dishes, made the bed, tidied up the house, packed a bag and left by the front door, leaving it unlocked. When Nils came home he would be disturbed if he found it locked; besides, no one in Hartford locked their doors, because there was no need to. She had to walk to the depot because Nils had the horse and buggy and was gone for the day. But Hartford was small and one could walk anyplace in a matter of minutes.

The bag wasn't heavy. There were only a few items in it, things she would need when she got to Sioux Falls. She would buy whatever else she needed when she got there. There was lots of money to be made in Sioux Falls. Everybody knew that. She was used to working hard and everybody knew that, too. She worked her fingers to the bone and had done so for almost ten years, slaving for Nils Nielsen, who never paid her the slightest mind, never showed any appreciation for what she did, never praised her efforts in keeping his house running smoothly and clean as a whistle, who entertained his friends and his large family, and who put up with his eccentric habits. She would show him. If she had to work that hard she was going to get paid for it, by golly.

Hartford, South Dakota, was a tiny hamlet fourteen miles northwest of Sioux Falls. The rolling land between them was farmland with scattered clumps of trees dotting the landscape. The fields were fenced off with barbed wire nailed to wood fence posts which lined the curving dirt road. A narrow bridge crossed Skunk Creek and it was a pleasant trip by horse and buggy if the weather was good, even though few roads were graded or graveled. However, rain turned the road into a morass. With the coming of the railroad, travel became easier and travelers could go from Hartford to Sioux Falls and back in one day in comfort in just under thirty minutes each way for the sum of 70¢ round trip. The train crossed over the railroad bridge spanning the Big Sioux River near the tiny town of Ellis west of Sioux Falls.

Gretchen was taking the train, the Chicago, St. Paul, Minneapolis & Omaha line. To get to the depot she had to walk through town and she wasn't looking forward to that, but as she walked she thought, and her thoughts were angry, overcoming her reluctance. She increased her stride. She was leaving Nils, maybe for good. He didn't need her. Any hard working woman could do what she did. And she didn't need him. She could manage by herself. Hadn't she managed all these years, managed without his support, his acknowledgement, his love? She had some money, exactly $7.43. She had saved it from the grocery money and from any other source she could find, even any loose change she found when going through Nils's clothes on wash day when a stray coin or two got stuck in the seam of a pocket. She had no qualms about keeping any money she found, because she needed it, and Nils never knew the difference, never missed it. Besides, he had plenty of money.

It was Saturday, a pleasant spring day. She was going to be too warm in her skirt, high-necked blouse and jacket, but it was too late to change. She would miss the train. Soon it would be May, the nicest time of the year, and she would surely miss Hartford, her home ever since she was a child. She would miss seeing everything turn green, seeing the flowers bloom, flowers that the women nursed so carefully, not unlike the effort of giving birth to new life in the sometimes arid soil, with the resultant beauty making it all worthwhile. She passed the Schmidt house and noticed the tulips were already standing straight and strong. They had all come up red even though Mrs. Schmidt had been assured there would be some yellow ones, too, and she could just picture her as she complained to the man at the hardware store, where she had purchased the bulbs last fall.

She walked past familiar neighborhoods with small houses set close to the ground. Some had porches on the front with slanted roofs supported by small pillars, giving owners a sense of having a broad veranda. Newer houses were two-storied, some with circular porches which extended to one side, indicating a more well-to-do owner. The tall, narrow windows, outlined with decorative brick, let in light without admitting the elements.

She crossed a dirt road and stepped up onto Main Street.

This would be the hard part. She had walked the same stretch countless times, but not with a suitcase in her hand, and if there were questions, which there were bound to be, although asked in an entirely friendly manner, she had prepared a ready answer. It was only a two-block walk to the depot. Main Street was bathed in sunshine, and it looked warm and inviting and homelike to her. What if this was the last time she saw it? It might be and it might not be she decided. She straightened her small hat, stuck out her chin and continued, quickening her pace. The sound of her feet on the wood planks that made up the sidewalk sounded very loud to her as she passed the Gage Hotel walking south. She was positive that everyone along the street would hear her coming and walk to the doors of their establishments and question her closely. But she proceeded past the implement shop with no problem. She stared straight ahead as she crossed in front of the blacksmith shop where the doors were wide open to the morning air. The blast of the forge hit her and she looked in. Jack Conroy was noisily hammering out a wheel for an early morning customer who looked up at her, smiled, stared at the suitcase and nodded a silent greeting. She managed a nervous smile in return and continued.

The buildings were connected to each other and to the wood sidewalk in front of them, each providing an economical dependence on the others, and Gretchen wondered how hot the hardware store must get with the forge going full blast next door, and her heart sank as she approached it. The striped canvas awning over the entrance to the hardware store provided shade and a welcome stop, but she couldn't stop this day. She also could not pass without returning the greeting she received from Mr. Nalor who was outside enjoying the fresh morning air, ready for any early customers. His shirt sleeves were rolled up and his heavy apron with pockets full of nails, nuts and bolts, and assorted bits of small hardware hung down around his hips. He was talking to several local men who had come to Main Street for their daily confab together and maybe a cup of Mr. Naylor's stout coffee which was always simmering on the potbellied stove. They lounged against the store front with its bold lettering proclaiming "Nalor's Hardware" with their thumbs stuck through their suspenders which held up their baggy pants. The men were past their working years and their daily walk to town was the beginning of an uneventful day. Some of them would find work on nearby farms soon for extra money and something to occupy their time.

"Morning Mrs, Nielsen," said Mr. Nalor with his friendly manner.

"Good morning, Sam," she replied as she kept on moving.

"Goin' to Sioux Falls today, I see,"

"Yes, I am."

She kept on walking, not wanting to answer questions, trying to overlook the curious expressions on the faces of the idle men as they considered the suitcase. She was almost to the Mundt Bank on the corner, halfway to her destination.

Almost every small town had at its center a building constructed of the pink jasper stone. The town radiated from that focal point and it was the building that housed the most prestigious business. It gave the community a touch of class and solidity, setting it ahead of any town without one. The Mundt Bank was such a building, a handsome two-story building with steps on the corner ascending to a large door with a heavy window. Steps also led down to a basement level. A big curved window on the main level faced Main Street and people inside were visible, busy going about the business of banking. Gretchen sighed. Nils had his money in there. She wished she knew how much. It was frustrating to try to run a house with all of his demands without knowing what she had to work with. She was about to cross the street when she heard a familiar voice. She froze.

"Why, hello, Gretchen. You're out and about bright and early this morning, aren't you?"

It was Adelaide, the one person she had not thought she would encounter. The woman knew everything there was to know about everybody in Hartford. Gretchen managed a weak smile and turned to face Adelaide Christianson who was coming down the stone steps from the bank, being careful not to touch the railing lest she soil her white gloves. She was dressed like she was going to address the local Ladies Aid, with her taffeta dress held tightly in the middle by a wide sash which was tied in a bow in the back, accentuating an already notable posterior. Mutton chop sleeves exaggerated her portly figure and her wide plumed hat was very out of place in the morning, but if she had important business in the bank she expected to look the part. Gretchen felt terribly tawdry in her modest attire and dismayed at the unexpected confrontation. Adelaide Christianson was the wealthiest person in town and lived on its outskirts in a fancy house with a porch that extended all around it. She was at the top of the social ladder, with what social life Hartford had to offer. She insisted that everyone call her by her first name, conveying the illusion of being as common as the rest of them, but coming across as less than genuine in her neighborliness. But folks complied, because she owned a great deal of the property in Hartford and it was best not to cross her, what with all the mortgages she held.

Gretchen reluctantly answered,

"Good morning, Adelaide. Yes, isn't it a nice day?"

"Going to Sioux Falls, I see. And with a valise. My goodness, my dear, why do you need a valise, if I may ask?"

She was on the sidewalk and peering at Gretchen curiously and suspiciously, with a glint in her eyes. Her perfume was expensive, but it had been applied with a heavy hand and Gretchen stepped back. She had to say her piece and she hoped to say it well, but she had not hoped to say it to Adelaide.

"Well yes, I'm going to Sioux Falls. I need to match some material and it's in the bag."

"I see." Adelaide was not convinced and she pursued the subject. As if it is any of her business, thought Gretchen.

"I'm making new curtains, you see, and it will be easier if I can show the salesgirl in Fantles how far I've gone and how much more material I'll need. I may even bring back extra material for new kitchen curtains."

The statement was not entirely true or false. Gretchen was, in fact, making new curtains and they were unfinished, but they were not in her suitcase.

She stopped her explanation, knowing she had said too much. There was no need for a lengthy explanation. After all, how many explanations had she or anyone else, for that matter, ever gotten out of Adelaide about anything? Or even Nils, who never told her anything either. She said, "You'll have to excuse me. I must hurry. Don't want to miss the train."

"Of course, dear," murmured Adelaide, as she stared at Gretchen's back, watching as she crossed the street. Gretchen felt her eyes boring into her spine, but forced herself not to turn around.

She glanced across the street at the women's ready-to-wear, the grocery store, and men's clothing store. All had their doors open to the spring air. She walked past the Opera House, the saloon with its stale smell of beer assailing her nostrils, and

Oaks and Babcock's place of business where motor cars were sold, all with awnings in place against the warm sun. Now and then the breeze whipped the redolent aroma of the livery stable around the corner just east of Main Street.

A few children were playing on the board sidewalk ahead of her but they scarcely looked at her. She smiled at them nevertheless; she had no children of her own and loved to see them at play. That was another blessing Nils had denied her. The happy laughter of the children was pleasant to hear and she knew they must be eager for school to be out in a few weeks when the boys could live in their overalls and go barefoot and the girls could roll down their dark stockings and do without their bonnets. They looked totally charming to her.

But she could not afford to dawdle or daydream. She stepped off the sidewalk and picked her way through the dirt path in front of the lumber yard and the grain elevators set next to the tracks. At last she arrived at the depot and stepped up to the platform. It seemed to have taken a very long time to get there, but in fact the walk took only a few minutes. At the ticket window Mr. Barber smiled amiably and asked, "Ticket to Sioux Falls, Mrs. Nielsen?" She nodded and he pushed it through the window.

"Seventy cents."

She was startled for a moment. She hadn't thought about buying a round trip ticket, but she always did, when she went in to shop. This was supposed to be a trip like all the others, so she gave him the money, lamenting the loss of 35¢, money she was sure to need.

"Train's about to leave; better get on board."

She took the ticket, murmured "Thanks," and walked to the train. The engine was puffing and spewing smoke, waiting to depart. Mr. Barber had not noticed her suitcase.

She got on board with new purpose in her step. She was not going to get all sentimental and look back. She might return and she might not. That would be up to Nils. She didn't know how he would react when he found her gone. She took a window seat and stared out the other side away from town, determined to not feel bad about leaving. The Oaks Funeral Home met her view. How ironic. Was her decision the end of her life as she had always known it or the beginning of a new one? She didn't know.

"All aboard."

The train began to move and she settled down to think and to ponder how her plans she had thought about for so long would work out.

The journey was a familiar one, one she and other women in Hartford took to shop in the city, and it was a trip they all looked forward to with anticipation. Goods were plentiful in Sioux Falls and there was a variety not found at home. The fun of new faces and a more hurried pace was exhilarating. The women who made the regular excursion had little enough to spend, but they needed little, needing more a change of scene, a change of pace. Train fare and a few dollars to spend made for a delightful day away from home. A treat before returning to Hartford was the routine, whether at a soda fountain at one of the drug stores or a heartier repast at Dickenson's Bakery and Confectionary, marking the end of a happy day, before boarding the train for the return trip home, laden with packages or not. Their men didn't object to the excursions, regarding them as harmless diversions, a small indulgence that paid off with better-natured spouses, more contented wives, made happier by having had a taste of the big city. They were always home in time to fix supper anyway.

Gretchen knew just what she was going to do when she arrived. She had it all figured out, having made her plans weeks ago, and she had everything down pat. She was familiar with the city from many trips in the past ten years. First she would need a place to stay, something reasonable. How she would love to stay at the Cataract Hotel. But that was out of the question. She hoped to find work there, exciting work from what she had heard, and they always needed help. But she knew she needed to find a rooming house close to downtown. It would have to be within walking distance. She had most of the day to find something and get settled. The last time she was there she looked at the rooming houses, sizing them up from what they looked like on the outside, when she and the other women hired a carriage just for fun and to rest their tired feet. Still, it would require considerable leg work and a decision had to be made before nightfall.

The sprawling farmland, sprouting green in all directions pulled a response from her. The open, rolling land, the wide expanse of blue sky with puffy white clouds were what she knew; it was where she had roots. Hartford and the prairie were her home, all she had ever known. She shook the thoughts from her head. She had outgrown all that. She was thirty years old and her life was stagnant, predictable and without meaning, with a dismal future stretching endlessly ahead of her. She would start over in the big city of Sioux Falls.

The time passed more swiftly than she remembered on previous train rides, and she heard the conductor's call, "Sioux Falls, next stop." She sat erect, closed her hands over the handles of her suitcase and purse and watched the outskirts come into view. Her heartbeat quickened. She was excited and a little scared but she stood up when the train ground to a stop. She left the car swiftly with the other passengers just as though it were another day away from home, except that this time she was by herself. She had not seen anyone she knew on the train. Some of the passengers had come hundreds of miles across country and were glad to debark from the noisy, jostling train at last. Gretchen realized she had paid scant attention to any of them and chastised herself for it. She might have seen someone important or famous. But since they had all gotten off together it was possible she might see them again.

The Chicago, St. Paul, Minneapolis & Omaha depot was on East 8th Street and it was too far to walk to where she wanted to search out a place to stay, so she splurged and paid her quarter to ride in a carriage that would take her as far as the Cataract Hotel. She shared the carriage with three other passengers, none of whom she ever saw before and she was filled with curiosity as to who they might be, but no one said a word and soon the carriage stopped at the 9th Street entrance to the Cataract where they all got out. The stood looking up at the large, imposing edifice full of activity and interesting people. All those rooms were filled with fascinating, wealthy people like those she had shared the carriage with and who had gone inside. They paid no notice of her when she did not also go inside. She knew that most of those in the hotel were probably living out their residency in order to obtain a quick divorce and that was troubling, although she had considered getting a divorce herself. After all, there were no children to complicate things. She would just have to wait and see. Right at that moment she had a long walk ahead of her, so she headed west up the sloping hill, past Main Avenue, Dakota, Minnesota, Spring and Duluth. She stopped at Summit Avenue out of breath. She mustn't get too far from town. It would be easier to walk down the hills to seek out a rooming house if she wasn't satisfied with what she looked at than to trudge upwards as the day grew late and she got more tired.

She stood uncertainly on a corner. Which way to go? She had never actually walked along any of the avenues for any length, only up and down 9th Street to get an idea the last time she was in Sioux Falls, when the women decided to hire the carriage just for fun. The houses looked bigger than she remembered and intimidating, and they lined the streets in all directions. They were far larger than any in Hartford. She turned round and round, reading all the signs which started "Rooms for Rent" or "Room and Board." Panic rose inside her, and she pushed it down firmly. Begin, she told herself. You won't get anywhere just standing here. Besides, you look funny out on the corner with a suitcase, just standing around. People will stare. Act like you know what you're doing, she told herself sternly. She crossed the street and climbed the steps of a house that looked promising.

# CHAPTER FIVE

# *The Boarding House*

Gretchen settled for a large house on a corner of West 12th Street. It had three stories with many rooms, numerous windows on all sides, a windowed cupola with a round pointed roof which gave it the appearance of a fairy castle, and a tall brick chimney in the center, which indicated a fireplace. Steps led to a wide veranda on the front and the back to entrances with stained glass windows encased in heavy oak doors. She was delighted with her choice.

Room and board was 75¢ a day. Paid in advance it was $20.00 a month, a saving of $2.50 and more, depending on the number of days in the month. Gretchen was thrilled at such a savings, but could pay for only one week, since she could not afford more just then. After her train ride, the carriage ride, and a week's rent, she was left with $1.23. She would have to look for a job the first thing Monday morning.But she was so tired and hungry by the time she found the right house and was shown to her room that she could hardly wait for supper and bed.

The boarding house was run by three sisters in their middle years, Opal and Josephine Gibson and Mina Jefferson. They had been left the house and a sum of money as an inheritance by their parents years before. They made a living renting the spacious house and its many rooms to boarders, providing meals with the assistance of a cook and Beulah, the hired girl, a large, heavy woman whose help became necessary as they grew older and their business increased. They had grown up in the house, along with three brothers, all of whom had moved away long ago and established their own homes and families. In the 1800s the house was home to a noisy, growing family with plenty of room for a multitude of cousins, aunts and uncles. As the years passed the house seemed cavernous as relatives moved away or died and there were left only the three of them.

Opal and Josephine were spinsters – maiden ladies is how they referred to themselves, genteel maiden ladies. Mina was the youngest in her forties, and she had married in the 1800s causing a stir in her family circle, because even though she was in her thirties at the time her fiance was a few years younger. In addition, the custom was for young women to marry in descending order of age, the eldest first and so on down the line. But Mina had always had spirit and was a rebel at heart and she prevailed in gaining permission to marry in the face of tradition, especially when it became apparent that her two older sisters had no immediate prospects. Her defiant ways came back to haunt her when her husband died soon after he left to serve in the Spanish American War. He had been a member of the First South Dakota Volunteer Infantry Regiment of Company C of the South Dakota Guards. The Guards departed for the Phillipines on May 29, 1898, upsetting those they left behind, because the war had ended on May 1, 1898, making any losses suffered all the more hard to accept. Mina had a sense of loss with no meaning, since it was malaria rather than enemy fire that had struck down her husband, leaving her embittered for a few years and a little guilty.

The widowed Mina recovered from her grief and rejoined her sisters in the big house and, when the inheritance money began to dwindle, they decided to join the growing ranks of others who rented rooms to transient strangers. In the five years since they had opened their home to others they had increased their bank account considerably. Room and board was a lucrative business and they were solvent and independent with the money derived from their many, ever-changing boarders. The divorce business had been a windfall for the ladies and, although they decried divorce, they rationalized that the poor, misdirected souls had to have a place to stay and The Lord had given them an opportunity to serve so, consequently, their guests received a little more for their money by way of some conciliatory, unsolicited moral judgments, especially on Sunday, when most of them found somewhere else to spend the day – after dinner, of course.

Gretchen was enchanted with her spacious room. Her entire house in Hartford would have fit into the third floor with room to spare. She had been given a room on the third floor, the only one the sisters had left, and it was a long climb but worth it. Through the lace curtains on her window she could look

Mina     Opal     Josephine

out to the south and the east with a good view of downtown Sioux Falls at the foot of sloping hills. She had a bed with a high head board, a large dresser that was big enough for several people, and it had a top of marble. She hung her few items of clothing in a commodious wardrobe, She would enjoy her stay in the large house. She removed her hat and jacket and walked to the bathroom at the end of the hall. She had been informed by Mina, with a certain amount of pride, that each floor had its own bathroom. She was shown which towel and washcloth to use which, though a bit worn, were still soft. The bath had a tub standing on claw feet, a circular basin with porcelain handles and a commode with a pull chain from a wood water closet high on the wall. If Nils could see this luxury he would understand her insistence of an indoor bathroom. There was room and a place for it in the shed attached to the back of their house. The outhouse got to be most uncomfortable in the extremes of weather, hot and smelly and full of flies in the summer and cold and miserable in the winter.

She took care of her toilet and went down to supper. She was famished. The steps were long and steep, but they were carpeted. As she descended she could hear the voices of others. Her curiosity was aroused and she wondered who they were, if she would like them and if they would like her, She reached the main floor slightly out of breath and walked through an arch which had a tall vase containing cattails on each side of it. In the living room the people ceased talking and all eyes turned to her as she entered. She smiled nervously and forced herself to proceed. Five people were seated in the room staring at the new tenant. They returned her smile and Mina met her, welcoming her with an outstretched arm.

"There you are, Miss—Oh dear, what is your name again?"

"Gretchen, Mrs. Nils Nielsen."

"Yes, of course. Gretchen, come meet our other guests. Everyone, meet Mrs. Nils Nielsen, Gretchen."

Murmurs of greeting rose and Gretchen valiantly tried to listen to Mina's introductions and to keep everybody straight. There was Enid Ferguson in her middle years, with proper manners and who was demurely dressed. The warm April day had heated the big house and she dabbed at her forehead and throat with a lace handkerchief. There was Dehlia Van Tassel in her twenties with a superb figure which she knew caught admiring glances and which she used to her advantage. Her auburn hair clung in ringlets on her forehead, but she appeared to be less warm than Mrs. Ferguson, as her dress was cut low and slightly off her shapely shoulders. There was Abner Faraday, an old man with numerous wrinkles with a neck like a tom turkey stuffed into a celluloid collar that did not seem to cause him any undue distress. He had long frizzy sideburns and rheumy eyes. There was Ignacious Wiggins, a man of indeterminate age, a diffident manner, an almost timid demeanor. His brown hair was thinning and glasses, attached to a fob originating from his vest pocket, were pinched to his pointed nose. Gretchen heard, "And this is Louisa Penrod. Louisa is employed at the Cataract Hotel here in town and has been with us for some time now."

Gretchen politely said, "Hello," to each of them and was spared any small talk when Mina announced, "Don' t sit down, my dear. Supper is ready. Come on everyone, supper."

Without further urging they rose and followed Mina. Gretchen looked around her and took in the fireplace against an inner wall. A door adjacent to it was open and visible were a pipe organ, several chairs with tufted velvet cushions and ornate carved wood trim, a black leather Morris chair in one corner, and a mahogany phonograph with hard rubber disks stacked beside it. Heavy tassled drapes at the windows gave the room an air of quiet culture, suitable for the pursuit of more ethereal activities and quiet reflection.

They entered a large dining room where a long table with a white linen cloth was set for nine, appearing to Gretchen like it was set for company. She was introduced to Opal and Josephine. Josephine was the older of the two, in her sixties. She was the largest of the three sisters and, despite her age, strong and capable. Her hair was white and wound in a braid above her square face. Her dress was loose and comfortable, as were her shoes which were, for a woman, of ample size. Opal was in her fifties, tall and slim with her graying hair pulled back into a bun. She wore spectacles and looked like a school teacher. Mina was in her forties and still an attractive woman of average size, with brown hair set in waves held back by combs. Her eyes sparkled and her warmth was genuine. She loved the people they had met in the past five years; she learned from them about the world, about other places and customs.

Gretchen learned that the three brothers of the ladies were

interspersed among them in age, with Josephine being the oldest of all of them. She ran the house with efficiency, gave the orders to cook and the hired girl, Beulah, who lived in a small room in back of the kitchen. She had no family and was content to live in the house and be on call at any time, being given room and board and a small salary for her subsistence. Opal took care of the mechanics of actually getting things to run smoothly, helping Beulah with the laundry and in keeping the guest rooms in good order. Mina was the one who kept the records of who came and went, deposited money in the bank, paid the bills and doled out salaries to herself, her sisters, cook and Beulah. Gretchen could see that she had chosen a very well organized place to stay while she worked out her problems. Josephine sat at the head of the table with Opal and Mina on each side of her. Everyone had a specific place to sit with one empty chair that evidently would be her place.

Delicious aromas emanated from the kitchen and she tried not to dig in too eagerly when cook appeared with a platter of baked chicken, followed by a mound of fluffy mashed potatoes, a gravy boat of steaming chicken gravy, buttered peas, assorted pickles, home baked bread, with chocolate cake for dessert. She was certainly getting her money's worth. She ate her meal with gusto, as did the others. When they finished, had their coffee and visited around the table, darkness was visible through the lace curtains at the wide windows. Gretchen grew sleepy, but she made herself listen to what the others were saying, fighting the desire to close her eyes. She learned that Abner Farady had been a guest of the sisters for several years, being their first paying guest. He moved in when his wife died in the late 1800s. Despite his emaciated appearance, he could take care of himself, needing only a room to sleep in and his meals. He spoke little in his thin, wavery voice, but enjoyed the conversation around him, conversation that changed with the guests who came and went over the years. He couldn't hear very well, but he knew all about the divorce situation and got a kick out of the various complaints he heard, mostly from the women.

The well mannered Enid Ferguson was, in fact, living out her residency to get a divorce, and had four months of the required six months to go. Gretchen wondered how any man could have brought her to such a decision. She seemed like such a fine woman. Now, that Dehlia Van Tassel was another matter. She chattered all through supper, flirted outrageously with poor Ignacious Wiggins who was so flustered he could scarcely eat and spilled his gravy on his shirt. Dehlia could not seem to stand a lull in the conversation and her constant talking began to wear on the rest of them. Mr. Wiggins, on the other hand, would not have said a word in any event, being so shy, except for an occasional request to pass a dish. He sighed, knowing he would have to put up with Dehlia and her chatter for five more months and he didn't think he could manage it. He could move, but the food was excellent where he was and the atmosphere was pleasant, plus he didn't want to have to start looking for a place to stay all over again. Louisa Penrod was nice and Gretchen took to her at once. Louisa was a few years younger than Gretchen but she was easy to talk to. What luck to have found someone who worked at the Cataract Hotel. Maybe Louisa could help her in her search for a job. She would ask her in the morning. Thank goodness tomorrow was Sunday. She was too worn out and emotionally drained to think about getting up and looking for work so soon. She needed rest and a good night's sleep.

At a given signal the sisters decided that supper was over and they got up from their chairs. So did the others; they excused themselves and retired to the living room. Gretchen offered her apologies, said she had had a very hard day and went up the stairs to her room on the top floor. Wearily she took off her clothes, put on her nightgown, pulled back the covers of the bed and fell in. Her tired body relaxed into the comfortable mattress. Upon heaving a sigh and closing her eyes, she was asleep.

She awoke with a start. What was that? Where was she? She had hardly moved and it seemed she had only just closed her eyes, so she was surprised to see sunlight coming through the lace curtains. Where had the night gone? She had slept soundly and well, but what had awakened her? There it was again. It was music wafting up the stairs, organ music. It was Sunday. "Rock of Ages" floated up to her, followed by "Onward, Christian Soldiers." She got up, visited the bathroom at the end of the hall and, much refreshed after washing the sleep from her eyes, she returned to her room and got dressed. "Faith of our Fathers" accompanied her descent and as she walked into the living room. No one was there. She glanced into the parlor and there they all were with the sisters. Opal was at the organ, busily working her feet on the pedals, evoking profound sounds of musical fervor to accompany her fingers as they deftly played the notes on the music set before her. The room reverberated with the tones of the grand old organ and she found it pleasing, but a trifle overwhelming. Opal had her Sunday dress on, a black silk gown with lace at the neck and the wrists. Her face shone with beatific peace as she played. Enid Ferguson waved a hand to an empty chair and Gretchen sat down. Abner Faraday was engulfed in a chair with his eyes closed, mouthing the words to the hymns, reliving a Sunday past which was obscure to the rest. Dehlia Van Tassel looked bored, but since there would be no breakfast until the concert was over she figited and waited. Ignacious Wiggins sat next to Louisa with an expression of stoic patience. It must be a regular Sunday ritual, thought Gretchen. She wondered if anyone in Hartford would miss her in church. Finally Opal finished, Josephine and Mina intoned "Amen" and then led their guests to the dining room for breakfast.

Gretchen's place was across from Abner at the end of the table. Louisa sat beside her. Gretchen didn't know how she could be so hungry after her wonderful supper the night before, but she ate her fluffy rolls stuffed with raisins and covered with frosting, scrambled eggs, and drank her coffee with cream eagerly. She could get used to not having to do any cooking.

It was Louisa's day off and she would get a chance to ask her about employment at the Cataract. But Louisa had a gentleman friend and she would be with him all afternoon. Gretchen decided to talk to her directly after breakfast.

"Why yes, they are in need of a maid, several maids in fact. Come in with me tomorrow morning and I'll introduce you to Mr. Simpson. I've worked there for three years now and he'll take my word for it that you are qualified for the job."

"Thank you, Louisa, thank you so much. I'm a hard worker, you'll see. I'll be ready to go when you are. I won' t keep you waiting."

Gretchen felt good. She had a good place to stay with fine Christian women who took care of every detail, she was filled with good food and warm companionship, and she would be able to pay for her room and board by the month very soon, saving herself a considerable amount of money. Things were working out just fine.

# CHAPTER SIX

# The Lawyer and his Client

Alphonse Grafton stood at the window of his office on the fifth floor of the Edmison-Jameson Building and looked across the street to the Cataract Hotel. The lettering on the glass in the office door read: GRAFTON & WILLIAMS, Attorneys at Law. The tall, wide windows were uncovered except for long, narrow dark drapes, which were scant enough to let in much needed light on the mahogany covered walls. A worn carpet with a fringe lay on the floor and heavy furniture lined the walls. His desk was set in front of the two windows plus a leather chair with its back to them. Anyone sitting in front of his desk faced the light from the windows, giving him a good look at any client held captive in the high backed chair which was too cumbersome to be moved by anyone who found its confines intimidating. Electric lights hung from the high ceiling and a paddle fan stirred the warm air. His client was late.

Alphonse Grafton was a portly man dressed in an expensive suit, complete with a buttoned vest over his paunch. He pulled a pocket watch from his vest, flipped it open, and muttered at the waste of his valuable time. He had several clients to see that afternoon and he was going to be late himself if she didn't make an appearance soon. Mrs. Grafton had planned a soiree for that evening and had impressed upon him the importance of his being home on time. He couldn't afford to back up his appointments much longer.

It was almost 3:15. The train would soon be pulling in, but he wasn't interested in any new arrivals that day. He was awaiting the arrival of Mrs. Clayborne whom he had been lucky enough to snag as a client, much to the envy of his partner, Jonathan Williams. He figured Mrs. Clayborne would soon be making her appearance, since he doubted that she would tolerate the crush of people entering the hotel at that time of day, of being touched by strangers. She had been aloof enough when

Clare Clayborne

Alphonse Grafton

she had interviewed him in her hotel room where she had found several calling cards of Sioux Falls lawyers, his included.

He replaced the watch in his vest pocket and stood with his legs slightly spread, his hands clasped behind his back. The early May afternoon was too warm for his suit and vest and the shirt with its tightly fitted collar over his broad tie. His jowls were slightly damp with perspiration, but his long sideburns covered up any evidence of it. A handle bar mustache lay across his face like a banner demanding attention. His hair showed no trace of gray and was parted exactly in the middle and combed carefully back from his round face. He was ready and waiting for his elegant, wealthy client.

At last she emerged from the 9th Street entrance of the hotel and proceeded to the corner of Phillips Avenue and crossed the street looking neither to the right nor the left. Mr. Grafton marveled at the confidence she displayed in managing to proceed in whatever direction she chose without looking to see if anyone or anything might possibly be in her path. Some people have a charmed life. He sat down in his big leather chair and waited, twirling his thumbs over his paunch. He heard the elevator door open and close, his office door open, low feminine voices, and then a tap on his door. It opened and his secretary announced, "Mrs. Clayborne is here."

"Good," he beamed, "Send her in."

Mr. Grafton rose as Mrs. Clayborne swept in. His secretary quietly closed the door behind her. Mrs. Clayborne declined to shake his hand, but permitted him to seat her in the high backed chair, murmuring a polite "Thank you." Her perfume rose to his nostrils as he made her comfortable. Beneath a small hat with a veil fluffed around its rim her thick brown hair was brushed back from her smooth face and held in place with stone studded hair pins. Lace of her high necked blouse accentuated her swanlike neck. She sat straight in the chair, but relaxed in her composure, and gazed at him with cool blue eyes.

"May I offer you a cup of tea, Mrs. Clayborne?" he asked with a conciliatory smile.

"No, thank you." She pulled off soft dove colored gloves. A large diamond shone on her ring finger. She clasped her hands in her lap where the ring nestled in the soft gray material that made up her fashionable afternoon dress. Mr. Grafton cleared his throat.

"Well, Mrs. Clayborne, I am pleased that you have chosen

45

the firm of Grafton and Williams to represent you. You can be assured that you will be accorded only the best of service, as well as all due speed in resolving your problem. However, you are aware that I shall have to ask you some questions, some of which you may deem to be somewhat embarrassing, but you may rest easy in knowing that anything you say will not go beyond these walls. Your case will receive the same discreet and completely private consideration that all of our clients receive and have received in the ten years we have been in business."

It was a familiar speech, one that was said with the same conviction as it had been said hundreds of times previously, but which always proved effective. Mrs. Clayborne nodded assent and did not appear to have taken offense. He went on.

"Now then, if I may ask you a few questions. What is your first name, Mrs. Clayborne?"

"Clare."

"Lovely, lovely." He was writing on a pad of lined paper, smiling and glancing up at her. "May I know your age?"

She answered without hesitation, "Thirty-seven."

Mr. Grafton expressed amazement. "I would never have thought it, Mrs. Clayborne. You look remarkably young, if I may be permitted to say so."

She looked mildly complimented and allowed herself a small smile without showing her teeth. Mr. Grafton forged ahead.

"You wish an action for divorce, which is what you told me when we spoke in your hotel suite. I need to know your husband's name, the date of your marriage, and the reasons for dissolving same."

"Edmund Clayborne and I were married in 1890 in Chicago, where we have lived ever since. Mr. Clayborne is in the stock exchange and we have lived well. Perhaps too well." She pulled a lace handkerchief from her velvet purse and dabbed at her eyes, recovered and lifted her chin. "We have a beautiful home in a good neighborhood and, as Edmund's business grew, so did our social standing. That required our rising to a better lifestyle – entertaining and attending fine social functions – so we needed some help at home in addition to our cook and hired girl. So I employed a maid, a sweet young thing."

Tears began to flow down Mrs. Clayborne's soft cheeks. Right on schedule, thought Mr. Grafton, but he made sympathetic clucking noises to comfort the lady and she went on.

"Edmund took quite a fancy to Anna,but I thought nothing of it. Edmund is a very likeable man; everybody likes him. I just thought nothing of it."

Her voice broke and she bent her head. She paused to compose herself and Mr. Grafton cast sympathetic cow eyes at her, waiting patiently for her to continue. She took a long, shuddering breath and said,

"As I said, Edmund took a liking to Anna, which she reciprocated I can tell you." The memory of it made her angry and she controlled her wavering voice to recite the travail of her marriage to this nice, courteous, caring man seated across the desk from her.

"I am sorry for losing my composure like that. I haven't really talked of it and when you asked with such compassion, you quite touched my heart, Mr. Grafton."

"Oh I do understand, Mrs. Clayborne. Some men are such cads. It pains me to think of someone as cultured as yourself having to withstand such treatment. Pray go on."

She gave him a weak smile, this time displaying perfect white teeth and setting her beautiful face aglow, momentarily dispelling its customary grimness. Mr. Grafton was dazzled.

"As I told you, we entertain many influential people and are, in turn, entertained by them, and I needed a maid to help me with my increased duties, duties which require so much more time and effort of a woman than of a man. Anna had been with us for about a month and I was satisfied with her, but more and more often I could not locate her when I needed her. She is young and I thought it was merely not being fully acquainted with her duties. But it wasn't that."

The grim look returned to her face and faint lines appeared around her lovely mouth.

"On one particularly tiresome day, after a very busy afternoon, I returned home to change clothes hurriedly for a most important function. My husband is well placed in the stock market you know."

Mr. Grafton remembered and nodded, concealing his eager smile beneath his mustache. He stroked it, his fingers following its upward curve, and listened as the lady told the rest of her story.

"I called for Anna several times and when I received no answer I went in search of her in somewhat of a snit. I pushed open the door to my husband's bedroom and there she was.

There they were, the two of them, together in bed completely disrobed. I mean, really! They didn't see me at first and I stood there dumbfounded. I fell back against the door and at the sound they stopped – what they were doing – and gaped at me. The looks on their faces were of shocked surprise, simply appalling!"

She was staring into space above his head, seeing it all over again. Mr. Grafton's imagination was running wild. He stroked his mustache with his other hand, watching her.

"Of course I ordered them both from the house and after I had a good cry and raged about a bit I rang up a dear friend, a confidante, and poured out my aching heart to her. She was wonderfully sympathetic and suggested that I come out here to Dakota excuse me, South Dakota, one does get confused about that. She said I could get a divorce speedily, in half the time it takes in Illinois, and the sooner I was rid of him the better."

Mr. Grafton said nothing, having heard it all before, in variations, and he knew when to remain silent. She went on.

"I am a good Christian woman, Mr. Grafton." She leaned forward and looked directly at him, her blue eyes flashing fire. "I come from quality people. I have been a good and faithful wife and do not deserve to be treated in this manner. We have to consider the children. We have two, a boy and a girl, who are presently with my mother in Chicago until I can return and take custody. It is terribly hard on them. They don't understand what's gone wrong and how can a mother explain about a father whom they love?"

Tears began again and the thin lace handkerchief was becoming quite damp. Mr. Grafton cleared his throat again.

"Of course we shall make arrangements for your full custody of the children. What are their names, please?"

"Theodore and Veronica."

Mr. Grafton was making notes on the pad of paper. "Tell me, Mrs. Clayborne, is there any chance for a reconciliation?"

She looked at him with the fire gone out of her eyes, now dull with tears. "None."

"Have you talked to Mr. Clayborne about this, of how you feel about his betrayal?"

"Of course not. What possible explanation could he give me? I could not listen to the reasons for his carnal behavior, his despicable actions. Furthermore, one wonders if perhaps

Anna is not the first—indiscretion."

So did Mr. Grafton. She had mentioned "Mr. Clayborne's bedroom."

"Well, my dear Mrs. Clayborne, if you are absolutely sure there is no chance of a reconciliation we can proceed with your divorce. I am sure you are aware that a six months' residency is required to establish that you are a citizen of the State of South Dakota. Immediately after that period of time we can serve papers upon your husband and you should have your divorce in a matter of days, a few weeks at most."

"I dread appearing in court and having my complaints heard by everyone present."

"My dear madam, have no fear. Divorces are handled in the privacy of the judge's chambers or, if in the courtroom, it is a closed court."

She was immensely relieved. "What a blessing, Mr. Grafton, but six months seems to stretch endlessly before me. And this is certainly not Chicago, this Sioux Falls."

"I can assure you that the time will pass quickly. The summer holds many diversions. Sioux Falls is a city of varied entertainments. In fact, I understand there is to be a ball at the Cataract next week."

"It holds no interest for an unescorted woman."

He looked at the beautiful woman seated before him and his thoughts were far from gallant, thoughts he had entertained with previous grieving divorcees. Perhaps he could pull it off again, although none had matched his present client's obvious class and breeding. Mrs. Grafton never knew of his dalliances and if she suspected he doubted that she would pursue any satisfaction in court, since it would be scandalous and he made an excellent living for her and the children. He knew she was not about to give it all up at this stage of their life together; she would overlook a lot.

He said, "Mrs. Clayborne, my wife and I attend these balls regularly. Would you consider being our guest for the evening? We would consider it an honor."

She gazed at her attorney with curiosity. It was becoming claustrophobic in her hotel room and she sorely missed the social life to which she was accustomed. Mr. Grafton seemed safe enough and his wife would be along. Her loneliness made her decide.

"Why thank you, Mr. Grafton. It sounds like a perfectly

charming arrangement."

She rose from the chair, her skirt falling gracefully around her, and he was around the desk in a flash, tending to her chair and bestowing upon her an obsequious smile as she pulled on her gloves. He watched as the diamonds luster disappeared inside.

"Very well, Mrs. Clayborne. Mrs. Grafton and I shall call for you at your suite next Tuesday at 8:00 o'clock."

She gave him her most generous smile in return, quite taking the breath out of him, then turned and left through the door which he opened just in time, and bowed slightly as she swept out. He closed the door and mopped his brow. His heart was pounding in his chest and he was becoming excited as a school boy and extremely pleased with himself. This one would surely be his most stunning accomplishment in his romantic exploits. He had not been at all sure that she would accept his proposal. He would thoroughly enjoy her company and pleasantly relieve her of $3,000 for his services, which she would gladly pay him.

A knock on the door was followed by the entrance of his partner, Jonathan Williams, a slightly younger, thinner man. He had a smirk on his face.

"Well, how'd it go?"

"Very well. Very well, indeed. Mrs. Clayborne is ripe for the plucking. Oh she will get her divorce, all neat and tidy, and I shall have a good time earning my fee."

"Alphonse, you old fox, I don't know how you get away with what you do to those women. I never get that lucky."

"It's all in how you handle these grass widows, John old boy. Treat them right, flatter them, fawn over them, and they'll give you anything – affection, money, anything."

Mrs. Clayborne left the Edmison-Jameson Building so buoyed up by her appointment with Mr. Grafton that she gave her maids the rest of the day off, causing them considerable consternation. Then she went shopping alone, walked instead of ordering a carriage, and she carried her parcels herself. That evening at supper she even condescended to ask her maids what they would like to eat before she ordered for them, throwing them into utter confusion. What had happened to their stern mistress to cause her to behave so out of character?

50

# CHAPTER SEVEN

# The Ball

The ballroom of the Cataract Hotel was on the second floor, taking up most of the area, with small rooms bordering each of its sides consisting of sitting rooms, places to relax and cool off when the heat of the evening made a respite from the dance essential, and where the "necessary rooms" as they were called, facilities for men and women, were located.

Balls were held regularly and were well attended, being a welcome relief from the boredom that inevitably crept into even the most determined divorce seekers, especially in the winter when South Dakota's frigid climate could be a cruel joke on those not familiar with winter on the plains.

It was a beautiful spring evening in May, 1904. The ball marked the end of a very pleasant day for the residents of the hotel, most of whom had spent it in the outdoors, creating envy in those in the city who had to work indoors, getting little comfort from the balmy breezes which wafted through every open window. The program for the ball proclaimed that the music for the evening would be provided by a nine-piece chamber ensemble that would play until midnight. It was made up of three violins, two violas, a cello, a piano, a horn and a drum. They would be playing the works of Mozart, numerous Strauss waltzes, plus a few selections, such as ragtime, that were more likely to accommodate the younger dancers who could do the sprightly one-step and turkey trot.

The narrow boards of the hardwood floor had been buffed and polished to a fine sheen, perfect for ballroom dancing. The large room had potted palms placed liberally along the walls. Long chandeliers hung from the ceiling, brightly illuminating the room. Yellow velvet tufted chairs and settees were interspersed along the foliage, giving onlookers and hopeful dancers a front row seat to observe the throng that would soon occupy the dance floor. The orchestra was seated on a raised platform at one end of the large room. Several couples were already engaged on the floor and the music of Johann Strauss, Jr. filled the room. "Tales from the Vienna Woods" greeted Alphonse Grafton and Clare Clayborne as they arrived and paused at the entrance. Mr. Grafton's face expressed his pleasure and Mrs. Clayborne appeared a trifle unsettled as she held a fan that she fluttered before her lovely face. Mr. Grafton touched her elbow lightly and they proceeded to the dance floor. He bowed to her and Mrs. Clayborne grasped the flowing skirt of her red satin gown and made a slight curtsy, bending her elegantly coiffed head just enough for Mr. Grafton to sneak an admiring peek down her low cut dress into her bosom, and they began to dance.

Mr. Grafton proved to be an excellent dancer, partly because he loved to dance and became proficient in the art, aware that he cut a fancy figure as he danced the waltz, the polka or the one-step; and partly because his portly figure gave him a nice bounce and a smoothness of movement that made him appear to glide. Mrs. Clayborne was impressed, surprised at her escort's sophistication. She was annoyed when he showed up alone. He was prompt, but Mrs. Grafton was not with him. He said he hoped she would forgive the change in plans, but Mrs. Grafton had taken suddenly ill and could not accompany him to the ball, but he could not in good conscience cancel the plans for the evening. After all, that would not be fair to her, now would it. Besides, he had really been looking forward to escorting her to the ball and alleviating some of the boredom she surely must have been experiencing since her arrival in his fair city. A woman of her breeding would have precious few contacts in a strange place and should not be ignored and left alone in such a time of need.

He had been so convincing and so contrite that she had agreed to go to the ball with him, although it bothered her somewhat to remind herself that she was going out with her lawyer, a married man, and that legally she, herself, was still married. But she was all dressed and ready and he was a good dancer. It had been a very long time since she had attended a social function of any consequence, and she, too, had been looking forward to the evening, to having a good time. Where was the harm? He proved to be a gallant escort, impeccably perfect in his manners, but his habit of stroking his curled mustache seemed a bit ostentatious. No matter; they danced waltz after waltz, whirling about the hardwood floor through the growing number of dancers. After each dance they received a round of applause, causing Mrs. Clayborne's cheeks to glow and Mr. Grafton's sideburns to glisten with perspiration. She begged for a rest.

"Dear Mr. Grafton, you dance superbly. How do you keep it up so? I am quite fatigued. Do you think you could fetch me a cool drink?" Her fan was fluttering rapidly before her heaving bosom.

He was off in a flash to the buffet where uniformed men and women served the multitude of dancers. Things were going very well. Mrs. Grafton would never know. How could she? She was in Omaha by now visiting her sister and she had taken the children with her. How she had fretted when he could not go with her, but he had insisted that his business just would not permit him to leave the city, that she should just go ahead and enjoy herself. He would catch up on some paper work. He would manage somehow. Ah yes, he would manage just fine. With cups of punch in his hands he turned to look for his dancing partner.

Mrs. Witherspoon said to her husband, "Did you ever see such a sight? Just look at that lawyer, that Alphonse Grafton. He's here with yet another of his divorcees. You remember her when she checked in. How on earth can he behave in such fashion? Waldo—?"

Waldo Witherspoon wasn't listening. He was watching, enraptured, as the dancers swept by in their fancy clothes, smiling, gliding in time to the swelling music of the ensemble. He was thoroughly enjoying it, keeping time with his feet, finding it hard to just sit there.

"What? Oh, yes dear. Do you want to dance?" He looked at her beseechingly.

"Dance? Why no, Waldo. Why do you ask me that every time we attend one of these functions? You know I never dance. It's unseemly somehow."

"But we always come and just sit and watch. Is that unseemly, too?"

"Never mind, Waldo. Would you get me some punch, dear?"

Obediently, Mr. Witherspoon left his seat, glad to get up and move around. He took his time on the way to the buffet, nodding and speaking to some of the people seated in the chairs along the wall. Then he amazed himself as he stopped before the chair in which chubby Mrs. Culpepper was sitting. She smiled amiably up at him, her round face pink with the warmth of the room, her feet clad in sturdy shoes swinging to the rhythm of the music. Her feet did not quite reach the floor.

"How do you do, Mrs. Culpepper. We have not met since you arrived. Allow me to introduce myself – Waldo Witherspoon. I wonder if you would do me the honor of this dance?" He bent over her and took her small hand.

She didn't hesitate. "Why yes, I'd be delighted, Mr. Witherspoon." She hopped down from the chair, her blue skirt swirling around her plump hips.

The encounter had taken only seconds, and in no time at all Mrs. Culpepper was in Mr. Witherspoon's arms, looking up at him and smiling happily as they circled the floor as the orchestra played "On the Beautiful Blue Danube." Mr. Witherspoon was not a large man, but he was taller than Mrs. Culpepper, and he felt like a giant as he led her in the waltz and she followed his steps expertly, all the while giving him her total attention, smiling happily up at him. They circled round and round and Mrs. Culpepper's full skirt ballooned dangerously to a risque height, giving onlookers a glimpse of ruffled pantaloons. Mr. Witherspoon lost track of where he had left Mrs. Witherspoon, but on one circle of the floor he thought he heard a faint "Waldo?" as he whirled past one corner where they had been seated beneath a palm.

His heart was pumping and he was having fun. He did not escort Mrs. Culpepper back to her chair after the waltz, but remained on the floor as the next tune,"Wine, Women and Song," was struck. How decadent. Mrs. Witherspoon would be furious, but at the moment he just didn't care. Mrs. Culpepper was as indefatigable as he was and they, too, earned a round of applause when the dance ended. He escorted her back to her chair, and seated a puffing Mrs. Culpepper, leaving her after deftly kissing her pudgy hand. He thanked her, stood with his back straight, and marched back to a very confused Mrs. Witherspoon. Mrs. Culpepper fanned her rosy face with her program, crossed her feet and swung them to and fro in her contentment.

Bart Kelly sat and smoked cigars, not really wishing to dance, enjoying the change of scene. He was studying the group of five women who seemed to be always together, and tried to decide if he should meander over and ask for a dance. All of them had flirted with him, knowing he was available, and they were all attractive, looking particularly alluring in their soft dresses. He made up his mind. He would dance with all of them. There was nothing like holding a pretty woman in his arms to aid him in a decision about whether to pursue her or not. Each of the women accepted his invitation to dance with alacrity, each continued to flirt with him in outrageous fashion, and he was asked the same first question by each woman in turn, "What is it you do, Mr. Kelly?" When he explained that he was in ladies' underwear their reactions were much the same – feigned shock and then laughter at his teasing, pressing closer to him by way of forgiveness. Mr. Kelly took the opportunity to explore their backs to see if they might be good prospects for his sales pitch.

Mr. O'Toole could be seen dancing sedately with Mrs. Anderson, after which they parted and disappeared.

Then Mr. McCallum stepped up on the slightly raised stage and spoke to the conductor who asked for quiet, as there was to be an announcement. All eyes were on Mr. McCallum and the ladies sighed with pleasure at his handsome appearance. He stood so tall and relaxed, so self-assured, nattily attired in the latest style for young men, casual yet smart. He smiled broadly at the group and began as they listened expectantly.

"Ladies and gentlemen, my name is Byron McCallum, as some of you know. My companion,with whom I am often seen, and I, wish you all to join with us in our happiness. Miss Alicia Cabot has consented to be my wife and we invite every one of you to come to our wedding."

Oohs and aahs greeted the news, everyone looked at the very happy Miss Alicia Cabot, who took her place beside him, and they clapped their approval. Mr. McCallum motioned for silence.

"We have not been in your fair city very long, but coming from the East we find your community refreshing. The residents are friendly and outgoing and we want to share our happiness with you. We shall be married in June in your splendid out-of-doors. An invitation for each of you will be left in Mr. Simpson's reliable care in a few days. Now," he said as he clapped his hands together, "I have asked the leader of this fine ensemble to play the popular "Maple Leaf Rag" by Scott Joplin. Celebrate with us. Dance !"

The orchestra struck up the lively tune and Mr. McCallum

and Alicia Cabot took to the floor to lead the spritely steps. They soon had the ballroom floor to themselves as the others watched, entranced, as the handsome couple moved as one, obviously loving every minute. The ladies sighed once more, this time in resignation, but they couldn't take their eyes off the happy couple. Applause was long and loud when they finished. Even the orchestra joined in.

More familiar tunes emanated from the orchestra and the floor was once more crowded with couples, delighted with the news they had heard, giving them something to look forward to with a reason to celebrate. The lights eventually dimmed as the music grew slower. Finally the ensemble played "After the Ball" and then "Good Night Ladies" when it was midnight, and those who remained on the dance floor reluctantly took their leave.

Gretchen was exhausted. She was not used to being up so late and working so hard. While the multitude of guests was reveling in the ballroom she had to keep the necessary rooms clean and in order for any who found themselves in need of the facilities or for those who might need assistance of any kind. She was on call along with Louisa to take and fetch anything guests might need from their rooms, for a cup of punch or perhaps a tidbit to nibble on. She began to resent the orders that were sometimes snapped at her, as though she were some kind of servant. Nils never snapped at her, just expected his house to be run smoothly and kept clean. But, she reminded herself, she was being paid well for her work as she moved around the crowded ballroom on her many errands, being bumped or stepped on, having punch spilled on her. Her patience was mightily strained. Actually, she was not getting anymore money for her extra work; it was just her shift and the ball happened to occur on her shift, but it was still her well-earned money.

"Isn't that exciting news!" exclaimed Louisa, as they tidied up the room and emptied the buffet table. "Just think of such a wedding. I'll wager it will be the talk of the county."

"I just hope it doesn't happen on my shift," said Gretchen with irritability.

"Mr. McCallum said it was to be outdoors. I don't know what arrangements that will entail, but we'll find out soon enough. Gretchen, you are tired, aren't you?"

She sighed and answered, "Yes, I'm beat."

Louisa was tired, too, but she was more used to it. "Don't be discouraged. You'll get used to it; it will get easier each time."

"I hope so. Right now I don't know if I can make it up the hill to the rooming house."

"Sure you can. Listen, we're almost finished up here. You go on ahead. I'll wind it up." She brushed aside Gretchen's objections. "No, you go on. You can do the same for me sometime."

Gretchen gave her a grateful, "Thanks," slipped off her soiled apron, pushed it down the chute and walked to the elevator. She pushed the button even though she had been instructed to take the stairs on flights of two or less, but she was just too tired to use the steps, even going down, and who would be in the elevator after midnight? The door opened and Ben, the elevator boy, gave her a tired smile. "Gretchen, step in. Had a hard night?"

"Hard isn't the word for it. I'm going home if I can make it."

"Sorry, but I have to go up first. Someone on 5th just buzzed and I have to get up there. Relax, it won't take long."

Gretchen squeezed herself as far into a corner as she could, hoping no one would notice her. The light in the elevator was not bright and she wouldn't make a sound. The door opened on the fifth floor and Alphonse Grafton got on, stroking his mustache and looking very pleased with himself.

"Down, my boy," he said. He didn't notice Gretchen, just played with his mustache.

The elevator stopped on the fourth floor and Ben opened the door. No one was there, but they could hear, "Waldo, I'll never, ever forgive you."

"But, my dear—"

On the third floor, when the door opened, they were startled to see Mr. McCallum passionately kissing Alica Cabot, who was limp in his arms, oblivious to the people in the elevator, as the door closed silently.

Ben raised his eyebrows and glanced sideways at Gretchen, but she was too tired to react.

When they finally came to a stop, Mr. Grafton got off and walked slowly through the lobby, whistling to himself. No one was at the desk, as Mr. Simpson had retired, but he left a sign by the bell to ring it if anyone needed assistance.

Gretchen said, "Thanks, Ben. Good night." She walked through the empty, dimly lit lobby into the cool night air and began her upward journey to her lodgings. She hadn't been this tired since Nils's entire family had come for Thanksgiving dinner and some had stayed for three days. But she wasn't paid for all that work. She would get paid on Saturday for another week of hard work at the famous Cataract Hotel.

She felt a little better at the thought and would have quickened her pace, but her feet hurt.

# CHAPTER EIGHT

# *Gretchen's Predicament*

Opal hurried into the large kitchen and whispered to Josephine, "Do you suppose we should invite the gentleman to stay for dinner? It's almost noon." Her tall, slim figure leaned toward her older sister for an answer. Josephine would know what to do; she always did.

Josephine turned from Beulah, the hired girl, to whom she had been giving instructions for the noon meal which cook had ready. She only cooked, leaving clean up to Beulah. The arrangement worked for both women and they got along well, with neither one interfering with the other's duties. It was a difficult decision for Josephine. Their unexpected visitor had caused a flurry of excitement at the rooming house. The regular guests were in the living room awaiting the announcement that dinner was ready when a loud knock was heard at the front door. Interest in who it might be caused all heads to turn toward the entrance with anticipation. No one was more surprised than Gretchen when Nils Nielsen pushed his way in and demanded of Opal, "You have a boarder here by the name of Gretchen Nielsen, do you not," said more like a statement of fact than a question.

"Why yes," stammered Opal. "Whom shall I say is—"

She didn't finish her query because Nils spotted Gretchen, who had leapt to her feet at the sight of him. She paled at his obvious fury.

"Nils," she said, "what on earth—"

He turned to Opal, who still grasped the door knob, her mouth open in astonishment at the rude man who had pushed past her.

"I want to talk to my wife alone."

Opal closed the heavy door quietly and said, "Of course. Please come this way. You will have privacy in the parlor."

He followed her through the arched entry, past the cattails

in the tall vases, and into the living room. He ignored the curious people who stared at him, and followed Opal's tall figure as she opened the parlor door. He glanced ahead of him into the dining room and observed the linen clad table all set for dinner before he turned into the parlor with Gretchen close behind him. He had not turned his head to see if she was there, but had taken for granted that she would be. He had not yet spoken to her.

Opal closed the door softly behind them and Nils turned to face his wife. Gretchen had often wondered if this moment would occur and had thought of what she might do if it did come, but now facing the tall, gaunt figure of her very angry husband she found she could not look at him. She had felt so secure in her decision to leave him and she had discovered that she could manage on her own and earn a respectable living. She lived in a clean, comfortable home and she had money in her purse. But at that moment she was frightened. She didn't know exactly why, just that she felt like a school girl who had been found out in some silly escapade.

In the kitchen Josephine made her decision. "It would be rude not to at least ask the man to join us for dinner. He can have Louisa's place. She is working the day shift today."

Beulah nodded and cook sighed, although she always made more than enough to eat for every meal. Neither woman felt the need for superfluous talk and they worked well together and carried out the wishes of the sisters exactly. After years of the combined efficiency of the sisters and their help, no one found it necessary to make a change.

But Mr. Nielsen was not to be their guest for dinner. After a brief, but loud argument, mostly on the part of Mr. Nielsen, much of which was heard by the occupants of the living room, Mr. Nielsen stormed out, bumping a vase of cattails on the way through the arched entry, making it wobble dangerously. He stomped through, slamming the front door behind him, making the room shake. Enid Ferguson stifled a gasp with her handkerchief. Ignacious Wiggins sat very still blinking furiously. Dehlia Van Tassel let loose with a hearty laugh, resulting in disapproving looks from the others, and Abner Faraday roused himself, opened his eyes, and said," Eh? What?" Gretchen could be seen in the parlor with her back to the door, her head bowed.

Opal took in the situation and said briskly, "Dinner is ready everyone. Come along."

Mina rushed down the stairs to see what the commotion was all about and saw that the residents had passed into the dining room and that the parlor door was open with a forlorn Gretchen still standing there. She entered the room and said sympathetically, "Gretchen, is something wrong?"

As she turned around Mina could see that she had been crying, but Gretchen pulled herself together and said, "Mina, please excuse me from dinner. I think I'll go up and lie down for awhile. I haven't been feeling very well lately."

"Of course, dear. You go right ahead. I'll make your excuses to the others. Perhaps you would like something later."

Gretchen nodded and swiftly left the parlor and climbed the stairs as fast as she could, but her strength gave out and on the last flight she was pulling herself along the railing. She reached her room and flung herself on the bed, lying there motionless until grief and fatigue put her to sleep.

Downstairs at the table, conversation was animated, led by the unquenchable Dehlia Van Tassel. Her auburn curls bounced as she moved her head from side to side directing her shrill voice to all as they began their meal.

"Did you ever hear such a fuss? Good night nurse, was he ever mad! He yelled at poor Gretchen about leaving him in such a fix at such a busy time of year on the farm, and of her leaving without a word, and without his knowing where she was. She must have asked him how he had found her because he raised his voice and said it wasn't easy, but he had finally tracked her down and he was going to take her back home to Hartford. Where on earth is Hartford?"

"It's a small town northwest of here," replied Josephine. She sat stiffly erect in her chair at the head of the table. "I don't think we ought to discuss Gretchen's problems. After all, we all have our problems now, don't we?" she said pointedly. Then, to change the subject, "I hope you all enjoy the berries. The grocer just got them in."

But Dehlia would not be quieted. "Gretchen must have told him she wouldn't go back with him, because he kept on shouting, telling her she was his wife and she very well would do what he told her to do and he wanted her home where she belonged. Furthermore, she was thin as a rail and running away like she did would do nothing except to make herself sick, to say nothing of what the people in town were saying about her. Then, I'll bet he grabbed her, because I heard her cry out like he was hurting her. Then they were both raising their voices and I couldn't make out anything else."

She finished, pleased with her recitation of what had transpired behind the parlor door.

"Dehlia, please," said Opal. "It just isn't right to discuss the business of anyone else in this house. And you were very rude to station yourself right outside the door listening like that."

Enid spoke up. "I feel sorry for Gretchen. She seems like such a nice young woman; she works so hard, too. But, come to think of it, she has looked poorly lately."

The men had kept quiet, but they had taken it all in with interest. Abner Faraday could hear better than he let on and missed very little if he could stay awake. He kept his thoughts to himself. Ignacious Wiggins found women to be very confusing and contradictory and had learned long ago not to venture an opinion concerning them.

Mina said, "I'll check on her later. Poor thing. She needs her rest."

After the meal the sisters gathered in the kitchen, putting things to right, making arrangements for supper. Beulah kept her counsel, but missed nothing of their conversation, merely rolled her eyes upward now and then.

Josephine moved around the kitchen slowly but efficiently, tucking strands of her white hair which had escaped into the thick braid around her head. "We mustn't interfere with Gretchen's affairs, but we can offer her our comfort and support and the assurance of The Lord's love. Maybe she has in mind to get a divorce and perhaps Mr. Nielsen will not grant her one. She has to make up her own mind and we have to stay out of it, not even discuss it."

The hot June day was wreaking havoc on the ladies' coiffures. Opal smoothed her graying hair into its bun and said, "I agree wholeheartedly. I'll play an uplifting hymn this Sunday, something with hope and bright promise. Music has the power to heal a wounded spirit."

"And you play so well, Opal dear," responded Mina, whose wavy hair only got more wavy in the humidity, making her look younger than her years." I often wish I had persevered in learning music, but I could never sit still long enough to learn anything. Mother must have become very annoyed with me."

"Annoyed!" exclaimed Josephine with a smile. "You were

sometimes an irritant to all of us. You just could not sit still for anything. But you do have a head for finances. We could not run this house without your expertise."

Opal smiled in agreement. "We three make a pretty efficient team, don't we? Each with her own duties suited to her talents. We can take care of ourselves and each other and not be beholden to anyone. Father would be proud."

Having uplifted their own spirits they went about their business humming softly as Beulah shook her head and rolled her eyes upward.

Later that afternoon Gretchen crept downstairs and out the front door without being seen. She wanted to avoid prying eyes, because she looked as bad as she felt. Her brown hair was limp and her cheeks were hollow. She needed to get out into the sunshine and cheer up. It was her day off; she would do some shopping and, she reminded herself, she had money to do it with. She needed to reinforce the reality of the independent life she had told Nils so adamantly she was now leading. Granted, she was thinner, but she worked very hard and she did a lot of walking and climbing stairs. She used up a lot of energy.

As she stepped outside and went down the steps into the bright afternoon sun she felt a trifle dizzy, but brushed it off as a consequence of not having had any dinner. She would treat herself to an ice cream when she got to the drug store. She walked to the corner and slowly down the hill to Phillips Avenue, the main thoroughfare, and found it crowded with shoppers, mostly women, in their nice frocks, their dresses of striped taffeta or soft linens. Large bows adorned their hair. Some wore wide brimmed hats decorated with artificial flowers or plumes. She fancied that many of them would fill the afternoon by spending their money in the fully stocked stores and shops lining the avenue, probably at Fantles Department Store or the Bee Hive Department Store. The women she saw exemplified what she aspired to be and she envied them. She had come to the conclusion shortly after her arrival in the city that it would be a very long time before she could afford to spend any real sum of money for anything besides the bare necessities. She did much window shopping and wishing. After her stop at the drug store for some necessary toilet articles she might just go into one of the more fancy places. She could browse and look.

She turned into Olson's Drug Store and the bell above the

door tinkled. She walked toward a grouping of small round tables set on curved metal legs and sat on one of the chairs supported by similar curved legs with a back made of metal in the shape of a violin. She would have her ice cream; it would provide her with some energy. She gave her order to a young waitress in a red striped uniform and looked around her. She often came to the store and enjoyed the friendly atmosphere. A big window near the door faced the west. The sun filled the room with a warm, cheery look, softened late in the day by scalloped awnings which provided shade. She didn't seem to feel the heat. Her ice cream was placed before her and she ate it eagerly, savoring the strawberry flavor as its coolness slid down her throat. She made it last as long as she could then, much refreshed, she got up and walked to the counter to place her order. Mr. Olson, the proprietor, was an older gentleman who had run the drug store for many years and he greeted Gretchen cordially.

"Hello, Mrs. Nielsen. I hope you enjoyed your ice cream. We haven't seen you in here lately."

"I've been very busy, Mr. Olson. Work at the hotel has been heavy the past few weeks."

"Ah yes, the divorce business sure picks up in the spring and summer, don't it? Then comes the winter and the grass widows leave in the snow and ice to what kind of future? It makes you wonder, don't it?"

"Yes, I suppose it does."

"Are you feeling all right, Mrs. Nielsen; You look a mite peaked."

"I'm fine, just tired is all. But I have a sort of stomachache. The ice cream did help, but do you have something for that?"

"Yes siree." He turned to the shelves behind him to the assorted bottles filled with dark liquids. "There's Magnetic Balm, but that might not be right for what ails you, being mostly for cholera, colic diarrhea or bowel complaints. Your children would probably use that." He raised his eyebrows at her.

"I have no children. No, I don't think that's what I need."

"Well, let's see now," he continued, running his fingers over the labels, squinting at them through narrowed eyes. "There's Schenck's Mandrake Pills for fever, indigestion, sick headaches, liver complaints, even typhoid. But I would think the typhoid would cause all of those symptoms now, wouldn't you? Now here's the thing. Perry Davis's Pain Killer for colic, cramps, the runs, spasms, heartburn, sour stomach—"

"I'll try a bottle of that. How much is it?"

"One dollar."

She checked her purse. "Very well. I also need some of that tooth powder." She pointed to an array of oval shaped cans. "And the Ladies Home Journal," she said on impulse. Maybe something current to read would take her mind off herself.

"Is that all, Mrs. Nielsen? Would you like this delivered or will you be taking it with you?"

"I'll take it with me. Thank you, Mr. Olson. I feel better already. I do like coming in here." She paid him and took the wrapped parcel.

She left and, somewhat buoyed, walked across the street to Fantles Department Store to look around. It was located on Phillips Avenue in the middle of the block between 9th and 10th Streets and was always filled with shoppers. She stood before the display windows for a moment, gazing at the garments attractively arranged, all in the latest style. There were also filmy curtains, soft fabrics and accessories to adorn a beautiful home. She sighed and went in. She reminded herself that she still had not matched the material for her curtains or even given a second thought about kitchen curtains, not seeing the need anymore. It would be fun to look and wish. She opened the glass door and went in.

Fantles Department Store was a long, narrow building. The walls were lined with counters with stools placed before them on which customers could sit in comfort while clerks waited on them. Behind them were small cabinets with drawers filled with spools of thread, embroidery floss, hooks, snaps, needles and the like. Counter tops had brass racks which displayed garments to the best advantage. Some of the more elegant garments were encased in glass cabinets. Tables containing dry goods ran down the middle of the room. The store hummed with exchanges between customers and clerks who endeavored to satisfy the merest whim. The sound of cash registers ringing up sale after sale was indicative of a very successful business. Gretchen longed to sit at one of the counters and have a clerk display some of their finest fabric or perhaps a dainty undergarment for which she would pay without first counting her money. But it would all come in time. She had money in her purse and each week it contained more. She had earned it herself and she had not had to ask Nils for it or search for loose change on wash day. She moved along the tables in the center of the store, examining the various cloths, feeling the soft nap of fine wool, the smoothness of lustrous satin, until her rough fingers snagged a particularly nice piece of green silk. She quickly withdrew her hand and hastened her step, hoping no one had noticed.

She heard a cool voice inquire, "May I help you, Madam?"

Guiltily she started and said quickly, "No thank you. I'm just looking," and hurried on. She prayed the clerk wasn't checking the damaged silk; she certainly could not afford to buy even the small piece she had snagged. She turned her head slightly to check and was relieved to see that the clerk had gone on to assist another customer.

She walked slowly along the tables to the end, turned to go back toward the entrance, all the while admiring the jewelry, the pretty combs and hair bows, and considered going next door to the Bee Hive. She reached the door, grasped the handle, and fainted.

She awoke in a white room, in a metal bed made up with white linens. A pitcher of water and a glass stood on a metal stand next to the bed and a green shade was pulled partway down against the setting sun in the solitary window. She moved, making a sound, and heard.

"Well, there you are, Mrs. Nielsen."

She tried to sit up. "Where am I? What happened?"

"You are in the hospital, Mrs. Nielsen. I am Dr. Edward Evans. Now you just lie back for a little while. You fainted in Fantles and a clerk arranged to have you brought here when she saw you collapse. Don't be concerned. You are just fine. We found your identity in your purse. Is there someone you want us to notify – someone who will come for you?"

"No, no one. Do you mean I fainted? I have never fainted. I guess I was just hungry; I skipped dinner today." She shook her head to clear it and looked at the doctor, clearly puzzled.

Dr. Evans peered at her kindly over his spectacles. "I'm afraid the reason you fainted was more than mere hunger, Mrs. Nielsen. I have examined you, but will need a urine sample to complete my examination. Then I will give you my diagnosis."

Gretchen was helped to her feet by a nurse who led her to the lavatory, and then waited in bed for the doctor. She fretted. She couldn't afford a doctor and a hospital. How silly it was to have been brought here, but she supposed the store didn't want to be liable. She would probably have to pay for the carriage, too. She sighed in exasperation. This certainly had not been a good day. Dr. Evans returned. His face was wreathed in a broad smile.

"Just as I suspected. You will be pleased to learn that you are going to have a baby."

Gretchen's mouth dropped. A baby. How could that be? She looked at the doctor in disbelief. "Oh yes, it's true. You are in your third month. Are you certain that we cannot notify someone for you?" His kind eyes looked deeply into hers which were brimming with tears. She swung from exhilaration and joy at the news to despair. She couldn't have a baby, not now. But she wanted one. What was she to do?

"Now, now, don't cry. I understand this has obviously come as a surprise to you. Don't get up. You should remain in the hospital at least overnight."

"But I can't. I have to be at work tomorrow. I am employed at the Cataract Hotel."

"I see no reason why you can't return to work if you take it easier. It is obvious to me that you have been working past your endurance. If you are worried about the cost, let me ease your mind. Your fee will be the same whether you leave right this minute or whether you remain until noon tomorrow. So I suggest that you just rest, have your supper, and in the morning we can see how you feel. Remember, you have more than just yourself to think about now." He smiled again with gentleness in his eyes and she felt much reassured.

She ate her supper eagerly and slept well. The next morning she sat in the lone chair in the room and ate a hearty breakfast brought to her on a tray. By the time she had bathed and dressed she felt more like her old self. The doctor beamed when he checked on her.

"That's more like it. Basically, you are a healthy woman, Mrs. Nielsen. You just need to take care of yourself. Perhaps you should give up this job of yours and just stay home?" His brows were raised in a question.

How could she explain to this nice man? She merely answered, "Perhaps. But I have to be on duty at 1:00 o'clock. Thank you, Dr Evans, for your kindness. I'll think over what you said."

He gave her a bottle of medicine for the relief of her queasy stomach, and he told her he hoped he would be delivering her baby when the time came, and dismissed her. She paid $1.75 for her hospital stay, $1.00 for Dr. Evans' services, including the bottle of medicine, and was delighted to learn that the carriage which brought her to the hospital had been paid for by Fantles Department Store.

"They didn't want any trouble," was the explanation given to her when she asked.

She felt a bit wobbly when she left the hospital and walked out into the morning sunshine. It was a new experience for her. she had never been a patient in a hospital before. She paused to get her bearings and looked up at the building. The Sioux Falls Hospital was a five-story structure located on 19th Street and Minnesota Avenue. She realized she would have to walk to work and that it would be a long walk. She wouldn't have time to stop at the rooming house to change clothes, but she had freshened up at the hospital and tried to arrange her hair in some semblence of neatness. She was fortified with nourishment and a good night's sleep and the doctor said she was a healthy woman, so she determindly set out to walk the thirteen blocks to the Cataract Hotel, the last three blocks being down hill. She arrived out of breath, yet exhilarated by the exertion her walk had demanded of her, and of the news she carried as her secret until she could decide how to proceed.

# CHAPTER NINE

# The Wedding

One day in early June the occupants of the lobby in the Cataract Hotel were surprised by the unfamiliar sound of a horseless carriage, a motor car, which was driven by a talented young fellow and parked in front of the 9th Street entrance. Some of the guests left their comfortable chairs and cups of tea to crowd through the doors out onto the sidewalk to get a better look at the brand new, shiny, two-seater Cadillac car. It was bright yellow with cream trim. In the forefront of those in the excited group surrounding the impressive vehicle were Byron McCallum and Alicia Cabot. The young man who had delivered the car safely to its destination climbed down with an air of pride and accomplishment and handed the keys to Mr. McCallum.

"It just arrived at the Milwaukee depot, sir, and I took the liberty of getting it out of the freight car and bringing it right over to you safe and sound. See, not a scratch on it."

Mr. McCallum ran his hand over the smooth surface of his new automobile appreciatively. He had not expected delivery, only to be notified of its arrival, but he was gracious about it and said to the lad, "So I see. Good work. It appears to be in tiptop shape and you spared me the inconvenience of going to fetch it. Here, something for your trouble." He handed him a dollar bill, causing a stir in the crowd.

"Thank you sir. Thank you very much, a pleasure to drive such a fine vehicle." He grinned and tipped the cap on his tousled head. "She rides like a dream."

Mr. McCallum took Alicia Cabot's hand, assisted her into the car, shut the door with a nice solid thud, and walked with a certain cocky air to the driver's side. He slid in, flung his silk scarf casually around his neck, and turned the key. The car sprang to life immediately. They waved to the crowd and were off up 9th Street hill.

Mr. Simpson

Mrs. Goldworthy

Mrs. Goldworthy, after making a note in her tablet, spoke to no one in particular, "What on God's earth is the world coming to?" and she returned to her comfortable chair in the lobby, her ponderous gait making her necklace ripple on her ample bosom.

Thereafter the betrothed couple were seen often in their car as they drove all over town, up and down the streets and avenues, waving to passersby who waved back after the initial shock of seeing such a dandy automobile in their neighborhood. They became a familiar sight as they cruised. They tried to stay on the few paved streets, but their adventurous spirits took them on many less traveled roads and they and their new car were often covered with the dust the spinning wheels stirred up on byways more accustomed to the hoofbeats of horses and the wheels of carriages. Upon their return to the hotel Mr. McCallum would park his prized possession in the alley in back of the hotel where he would carefully wipe it off, dust the interior, and cover it with a heavy cloth to protect it from the elements.

The couple appeared to be the epitome of carefree, devil-may-care youth, but they were also making serious wedding plans. Soon the hotel guests found invitations in their cubicles behind the reservation desk, along with their keys. Invitations were also posted or distributed personally to acquaintances they had made during their stay in Sioux Falls, younger people, some who were married couples, some who were getting a divorce. They even had the invitation published in the Daily Argus Leader, implying the more the merrier:

Mr. Byron McCallum and Miss Alicia Cabot
of Massachusetts
request the pleasure of your company
as they recite their wedding vows
on the 23rd day of June, 1904,
at the hour of 2:00 o'clock in the afternoon
on Seney Island, Sioux Falls, South Dakota.

A reception will be held on the island
immediately following the ceremony.

In case of inclement weather
the ceremony and reception will be held
in the ballroom of the Cataract Hotel.

No Gifts Please

71

Seney Island was a 10 acre tract in the Big Sioux River above the Falls. It extended west to North Phillips Avenue close to the Chicago, Milwaukee & St. Paul depot on 5th Street. It was an irregular tract of land, a community park privately owned by a George Seney, the investor instrumental in building the ill-fated Queen Bee Mill. It was indeed an island, a popular picnic area which was grassy and heavily wooded, with an aura of a sylvan woods out in the country secluded from the noisy city, but which was in fact close to the downtown district. Picnickers enjoyed breezes wafting through the thick branches of the massive trees and the cooling shade provided by them. Although it was close to the city proper it could not be reached except by boat. At the foot of 9th Street was a dock where boats could be rented for 35¢, 50¢ if someone from the boathouse rowed a patron and party across. A steam launch was also available, more costly, but larger and more roomy. A large dance pavilion was located near the dock and during the summer months and far into the fall the hall would reverberate with rousing music and the voices of revelers, dancing the night away.

The Big Sioux River wound around the city, providing access to the pleasures of recreation on the water to the residents of the city, pleasures much appreciated on the prairie. Steam powered launches, flatboats in reality, were available which held a dozen or more passengers. They were protected from the sun by bright awnings as they traversed the river on Sunday afternoons. They were a familiar sight as they chugged up and down the river, perhaps stopping for a relaxing interlude on Seney Island. Some people rented rowboats; suitors rowed in leisurely fashion up and down the river as their comely companions lay back on pillows in comfort, shaded by a frilly parasol. The launches and boats could travel south to Second Island near 26th Street and feel truly isolated when the city disappeared in the distance, yet without being very far from its comforts.

Recipients of the wedding invitations were immensely flattered, feeling singled out and not part of the crowd who would attend the wedding merely as the result of reading the invitation in the paper.

Mr. Witherspoon was reading the mail and came upon the opened invitation which had been carelessly flung aside by his wife.

"My dear, how nice. That young couple has invited us to their wedding."

"Yes, along with the entire population of Sioux Falls. Quite improper."

"But, we are going, aren't we?"

She put down her embroidery and sighed. Maybe the whole affair was totally improper, but the invitation was enticing. The summer was stretching endlessly ahead of them, their room seemed to grow hotter by the day, and how better to see for herself just what was what and dispel the rumors floating about. Her curiosity was definitely piqued.

"We'll see what kind of day it is," she said. "I don't want to get all ruffled by the wind, Waldo. Have you noticed how the wind seems to blow constantly in this place?"

Bart Kelly had returned to the hotel after spending the day in East Sioux Falls to find his invitation in his cubicle. Older than the present City of Sioux Falls, East Sioux Falls held a poor reputation of being a rough, undesirable area where a lower class of people lived, There was much drunkenness and brawling. Bart Kelly had discovered games of chance in the area with a slightly dangerous edge – dog fights. He had seen cock fights aplenty, but the dog fights which were held regularly, and the bloody, vicious carnage of two ugly dogs locked in a duel to the death held a fascination for him. He came out a winner more often than not but, even so, his presence and his thick wallet were always welcome on the east side.

He concluded it would be more enjoyable to attend the wedding with a companion and couldn't decide on which of the many lonely divorcees to bestow his company, so he decided to take as his guests the three remaining women from the original five who had been inseparable during their stay at the Cataract. He had sold each of them corsets of varying degrees of snugness, plus some hosiery, convincing each of them that hers was the most beautiful form he had ever fitted, all with great propriety of course, over the lady's chemise with a woman who accompanied him for the fitting. In turn, he was later rewarded for his gallant efforts and flattery with a bit of romance, money for the undergarments, and feminine companionship whenever he wanted it. Somehow, his multiple companions who accompanied him on his excursions did not mind the presence of the others, such was the personality of Bart Kelly. Even though he fancied big, smelly cigars and loud clothing, particularly garments with lots of checks, the women gladly accepted his invitations. What Bart Kelly took as im-

73

mense attraction to his manly charms was only the availability
of an escort for the lonely, bored women, an escort with a bot-
tomless purse who didn't mind spending money on them, who
knew they would soon be leaving Sioux Falls with their divorce
decrees, as had their two predecessors. They were a noisy party
returning to the hotel to find an envelope for each of them.
"Well ladies, it looks like we've been invited to a wedding.
I'll pick you up at 1:30 on the 23rd."
"Thanks honey; 'bye." they said in unison and, giggling,
entered the elevator to go to their rooms.

Mr. O'Toole asked Mrs. Anderson to accompany him to
the wedding and assured her it would all be very correct, since
it was a public function held on an island where a hundred
or more guests would be assembled. They discussed it seated
in the hotel lobby as they opened their invitations along with
the others. Mr. O'Toole made no attempt to keep his asking
her private. She agreed to go with him. No one heard their
words as the room was abuzz with conversation at the pending
event.

Mrs. Culpepper grinned broadly and watched the others
in the room as she tucked her invitation into her purse.

That night in the kitchen, as the bellhops and maids had
their supper, the talk centered on the wedding.

"Isn't it exciting, Billy?" exclaimed Louisa. "Isn't it the most
romantic thing you ever heard?" Her excitement was catching
and the others agreed that it would be the wedding of the year.

Mike said, "Yeah, let's hope the weather holds. Ya never
know what it's goin' to do. Could be a tornado whips through."

A maid countered, "Not likely in June this late. It could
rain though. I' d think it would be lots easier to hold the whole
thing right here than to cart everything to the dock to transport
over to the island, set it up on that uneven ground, and then
haul it all back here."

Hank said with his mouth full," It's only a block to the
dock. Won't be hard."

Louisa continued, "Do you think all the hotel guests will
be there, Billy? And what about the people in town? How many
are expected? There wasn't even an RSVP on the invitation.
How is the staff to know how many to plan for, for goodness
sake?"

Billy laughed and said, "Don't worry your pretty head about
it. I'm sure we'll have some idea of how many people to plan

for. Besides, it will be informal and people will expect to fend for themselves to some extent."

He looked with fondness on her, her cap askew as usual, with her dark curls bobbing. They gazed into each other's eyes, not putting into words what they were thinking, but it was not lost on those at the table, and they all burst out laughing.

"We know what you two are thinking, don't think we don't."

"Your turn will come soon enough."

"Enjoy your freedom while you can. You're married a long, long time, you know."

"Unless you decide to get a divorce."

This remark was booed down. Gretchen sat quietly, taking in the talk around the table. So far, no one had taken notice of her condition, but her condition was not yet noticeable. The sisters at the rooming house had commented on how much better she was looking, of how she had "picked up" in the last few weeks, but no one had the slightest idea of her dilemma.

Louisa went on. "That Mrs. Clayborne has certainly been perky lately. Even her personal maids have told me, in the strictest confidence naturally, that she has been much more agreeable and not so picky. And do you know what else they said?" she whispered, and everyone leaned forward to catch every word. "Well, Mrs. Clayborne has been seen in the company of that Alphonse Grafton more than once. You remember them at the ball, how they danced together all evening. This lawyer fellow is married, but no one ever sees him with his wife, but he has been seen with Mrs. Clayborne and she doesn't seem to mind one whit."

Louisa settled back, satisfied with having impressed her listeners, who whispered to one another at this newest tidbit of gossip, adding some tidbits of their own that they had learned in the course of their duties. Gretchen felt a bit appalled at Louisa's gossipy ways, but still intensely interested in what she always had to say. She tried to deny her interest, but the juicy gossip that made the rounds of the table every night captured her attention. Nothing like this ever happened in Hartford, not that she knew anyhow. Life in Sioux Falls, combined with her work at the Cataract, was fast-paced and full of a variety of unique people, folks she would never have even heard of if she had not come to the city. Yet at that moment she wanted to be home in Hartford, to be with Nils and to be surrounded by familiar sights, sounds and smells, to await the birth of her baby, an unexpected gift that she had given up hope of ever having. Maybe she should write to Nils and ask his forgiveness. But how could she tell him about the baby now? He might be angry or, worse, suspicious. She would wait awhile longer to make up her mind about what to do.

At the rooming house the sisters were discussing the upcoming nuptials. Josephine remarked, "An announcement in the paper is really gauche. Can't you just imagine those who will attend merely from reading about it?" She moved her large frame slowly, checking the cooking pots on the big black kitchen stove hot with wood chunks, and conferring with cook and Beulah. The room was warm.

Opal wasn't that sure. "It is unusual, but it should be nice out there in the fresh air like that. But of course we won't be going – will we?"

Josephine shot her a disapproving look and Opal added, "Of course we won't."

But Mina was not convinced. "I just think you two are jealous because we didn't receive an invitation in the mail. I happen to think it would be a grand affair to attend. What fun to be on the island with the reception in the shade under those wonderful trees. What do you think? Couldn't we go? Really, what harm would there be?"

Josephine turned from the stove and said sternly, "It would definitely be improper to even consider attending such a loosely put together affair. I suggest that you put it out of your minds, both of you." Opal said nothing, but Mina bristled. She might just go anyway. Beulah rolled her eyes upward and laid out the serving dishes. Cook announced to the sisters, "Supper's ready."

Supper was a lively meal with everyone talking about the wedding. Dehlia Van Tassel announced loudly exactly what she would be wearing. Enid Ferguson thought she might go as it would be a pleasant way to spend the afternoon. Abner Faraday and Ignacious Wiggins glanced at each other briefly and said nothing. They would enjoy the empty house all to themselves with some peace and quiet.

June 23rd came in a bright blaze of sunshine and it was evident that the wedding would take place on Seney Island as planned. A cooling breeze filled the air and there wasn't a cloud in the sky. Mr. McCallum and his bride to be were seen leaving the hotel shortly before noon, getting into the shiny Cadillac and driving south on Phillips Avenue. Mr. Simpson was a nervous wreck. Any entertainment that was held in the hotel was reason enough for him to be nervous and it caused the left corner of his mouth to twitch. His rosy lips grew more crimson and his thin mustache was in constant movement. But he was an efficient man and any event under his supervision always went off perfectly. However, this wedding was an immense undertaking, and for it to be held on Seney Island was going to be a tremendous effort. It could be done, but what an inconvenience to him and the guests. The guests might have given him an argument on that point, because most of them were looking forward to it with immense anticipation and they would be in attendance.

Several loads of tables, chairs, silverware, dishes, linen cloths and the like were already being dispatched on a large enough flatboat that had been located from someone downstream. The men in charge of transporting the cargo were in extremely high spirits and Mr. Simpson was sure that some of the hotel's fine furniture would be dumped into the Big Sioux River and lost forever. Furthermore, the undue noise because of the festive occasion was driving him mad. To watch as the bride and groom drove off in that fancy car of theirs only added to his distress. They would undoubtedly be late for their own wedding, causing all concerned needless worry. Such irresponsibility! There was too much confusion over a wedding between a couple from a state that very few people knew anything about. Foreigners, that's what they were, upsetting his expertly run organization. Mr. Simpson's mouth was twitching rapidly and he turned his back to arrange the keys in their cubby holes lest anyone see how distressed he was becoming.

Mr. Simpson's inner turmoil was all for naught because everything went smoothly. The bride and groom reappeared, having been gone briefly to attend to some last minute detail with the minister. They immediately got dressed in their wedding finery and reappeared in the lobby which was crowded with onlookers who had waited for them. The couple walked the short distance from the hotel to the bottom of 9th Street, leading a procession of those in the lobby. They stepped into a gaily decorated steam launch at the dock and were conveyed to Seney Island in a few minutes without incident, where they could still hear the applause from those on the dock who would soon follow them.

The townspeople who were there to attend the wedding were dressed in their Sunday best. They filled boat after boat and made a happy bridal procession as one by one they landed on the island. The boathouse owner was ecstatic as he counted up his increasing proceeds. What a great idea, having a wedding on the island. Mr. Simpson had outdone himself this time was the prevalent thought as the man smiled broadly and waved boats into the river, all laden with well dressed passengers in a joyous frame of mind.

The guests assembled under the trees. The sun was directly overhead and, though the day grew warm, the sun's rays were diffused into a lacy pattern on those gathered below. Most guests were required to stand through the short ceremony because of the lack of space for any accumulation of chairs, but no one minded. Local dignitaries, including the mayor, sat in front. A raised platform stood at the end of a clearing and a minister dressed in a loose white robe waited in readiness. When the boats had delivered all the guests and the island was filled with merry onlookers, Mr. McCallum appeared resplendent in blue trousers, a white cutaway and a crimson cumberbund. His blond hair was carefully combed and he looked like a prince from some fairyland, so handsome that the women emitted one collective sigh at the sight of him. A spinet was playing at the rear of the platform and its tinkling tones were carried to everyone on the island by the balmy breeze that played through the verdant trees.

The crowd quieted expectantly, the woman at the spinet swung into Lohengrin's Wedding March, and all eyes were on the bride as she walked slowly down a path which had been covered with a white cloth so her dress would not be soiled as it trailed behind her. She was stunning in a pale pink gown with a slight bustle and long sleeves which tapered to a point on her slim hands which held pink roses. A soft wide brimmed hat with a short veil covered her long, fair hair which fell to her shoulders in soft curls. Above the scooped neck of her soft dress there hung from her lovely neck a heart pendant surrounded and outlined with diamonds which sparkled from every facet from the filtered sunshine. She looked straight ahead to her beloved with love in her happy smile.

Subdued voices and whispers could be heard at the sight of her, but they ceased as the minister began his sermon, a sermon which proved to be brief and to the point. Then the vows were said with the bride giving herself completely to her husband, with spoken words of her own promising to love and trust him forever. Mr. McCallum, in turn, repeated his vows, with additional words of his own, promising to love her and giving her freedom for her own interests during their marriage, which caused a murmur from the crowd. He placed a ring on her finger which was so brilliant that gleams of light danced all around them, creating an even greater stir. Then the groom kissing his bride with passion and the murmur swelled to a loud shout of approval and spontaneous applause. Mr. and Mrs. McCallum turned to face their guests with happy smiles. The spinet sounded a spirited recessional as they walked down the white cloth to the reception table, acknowledging the well wishers on both sides.

"Well!" said Mrs. Witherspoon to her husband, "That was certainly as scandalous a display as I have ever seen. Don't you agree, Waldo? Waldo —?"

Waldo wasn't there. He had left her side and she had not noticed, having been more engrossed in the proceedings than she admitted to. Now where could he have gone? She wanted some punch and then go back to the hotel.

The pretty ceremony had moved Gretchen to tears. She quickly wiped her eyes and straightened as the guests surged toward the refreshment table, led by the radiant bride and her groom. She looked into the happy face of the new Mrs. McCallum, who smiled at her in a friendly manner. Gretchen handed her a knife decorated with a pink ribbon with which to cut the tiered cake which was covered with pink and white rosettes. It would be up to her to cut the rest of it for the multitude who all wanted a piece of the beautiful wedding cake. She and Louisa worked efficiently side by side, dishing up the cake, while other maids poured punch and coffee. They were so busy and the milling crowd was so thrilled to have been a part of such a prestigious occasion that no one noticed clouds forming until the darkening sky made it clear that the weather was changing. Mr. and Mrs. McCallum hurriedly and heartily thanked everyone for coming to their wedding and for making it such an auspicious day, then suggested that they all leave the island before it started to rain and led the way to the shore. The bedecked boat was waiting for them and the bride and groom led the string of boats back to the dock at the bottom of 9th Street. Raindrops splattered on the river and they stepped onto the dock just as the sprinkles began in ernest. Laughing playfully, the bride picked up her skirts, took the arm of her husband, and they ran up 9th Street, getting soaked in the process, followed by a hundred or so wet revelers who joined in the laughter as they swarmed up the sidewalk and filled the street as well as their Sunday clothes which were thoroughly drenched. They were led by the boisterous Dehlia Van Tassel in her revealing bright blue satin gown, her bosom jiggling precariously in the low cut bodice, as her auburn hair streamed behind her.

Mrs. Clayborne's sense of humor did not extend to getting wet. "Mr. Grafton, you said a carriage would be waiting for us when we returned," she shouted over the noise of the swelling crowd.

It was obvious that there was no carriage, nor would there have been any room for one with all the people emerging from their boats and racing up the middle of 9th Street.

Mr. Grafton said, "My dear Clare, I suggest that we make a run for it."

Whereupon he took her arm and they scurried up the street as fast as Mrs. Clayborne's decorum would permit.

Mr. Simpson was not amused when his lobby filled with soggy, noisy people, half of whom were not even guests of the hotel, tracking in mud and water onto his carpet. The elevator held only the bride and groom while most of the others ran up the stairs to their rooms to dry off and change their clothes. The remainder stayed, looked around the lobby with interest as the bride and groom disappeared from view, and waited for the rain to stop.

"This modern generation will be the death of me," muttered Mr. Simpson in exasperation.

Mrs. Clayborne was distinctly unhappy about the entire situation when she arrived at last with an apologetic Mr. Grafton puffing at her side.

"My dear Clare, let me escort you to your suite. You will be dry in no time. After all, it's only rain. And might I say that you look completely charming."

She glared at him as they waited for the elevator. Water was dripping from the brim of her large hat onto her damp bosom. "Mr. Grafton," she said coolly, "I'm perfectly capable of getting to my room by myself. You must leave now please. I am sure Mrs. Grafton will be waiting for you since she is

Dehlia

not feeling well. Please give her my regards. Thank you for a lovely afternoon."

She swept into the elevator which, fortunately, was empty because she didn't look to see. How humiliating, she fumed to herself, to be seen in such a disgraceful state, utterly soaked to the skin. She was speedily carried to the fifth floor by Ben, the elevator boy who stared straight ahead.

Conversation at the supper table at the boarding house that night was loud and lively despite Josephine's attempts to change the subject. As usual, Dehlia Van Tassel kept up a steady stream of comments, all of which were listened to with interest by Abner Faraday and Ignacious Wiggins who, even though they had remained at the rooming house that afternoon, were nonetheless intrigued by all of the goings-on.

"You should have been there," she said to Mr. Wiggins, giving him a poke on the arm, causing him to spill a spoonful of peas in his lap, "It was just wild, I mean what a show! The bride was gorgeous, of course. But you know what they say – all brides are beautiful. But I wonder, since they've been in town so long and being together all the time and all, if she's –" She stopped abruptly as Josephine and Opal looked at her in shock and disapproval and quickly cleared their throats.

"Well, you know what I mean. And she didn't wear white, you know. That pink dress really stood out, didn't it? Anyway, you ought to have had a gander at the groom. Now there is a handsome man. All the women were in a flutter over him, I can tell you."

Mina said, "Yes, but weren't they a sweet couple. And their vows were so unusual, so untraditional."

Opal exclaimed, "Do you mean to say that you went to the wedding after we all discussed it?"

Mina tossed her head, her hair very wavy from the rain, and said, "Yes I did. It was an open invitation. But I stood; there weren't many chairs – just enough for the important people in town. Mayor Burnside was in the front row. Wouldn't his presence make it respectable?"

"Really!" spoke Josephine.

Enid spoke up. "Did you ever wonder what those two are doing out here all the way from Massachusetts in the first place? It's odd that they would come so far out to the plains to be married."

That was a thought which made them all ponder.

The rain continued and thunder rumbled across the leaden sky for the rest of the afternoon. The transport back to the hotel of the wedding paraphernalia became a matter for mirth and the flatboat was filled with stocky workers who filled the empty river with loud, bawdy songs, but who managed to get the furniture and other items back in one piece, being only slightly warped from the rain. "Blow the Man Down" came floating up the hill to the Cataract. Mr. Simpson wondered what had been added to the wedding punch. Despite Mr. McCallum's generous tip, Mr. Simpson vowed to never again engineer a wedding or any other outing, for that matter, on Seney Island.

Any cleanup of the lobby and stairs would have to wait until morning. There would be diners coming down to supper soon, all agog with talk about the afternoon's affair, and there would be no useful purpose served in beginning any cleanup now. He was grateful that the day was nearly over. He was therefore surprised to see a tall, stocky man enter the lobby and approach the desk. He had presumed that all the train passengers had long since arrived and were in their rooms and he dreaded having to recite to another stranger the reason for the disreputable appearance of his once immaculate lobby. But the man appeared not to notice. His gray mustache and Vandyke beard could not hide the man's grim demeanor. His felt hat was damp and he looked tired and uncomfortable. As he approached, Mr. Simpson noted that the man leaned heavily on a sturdy walking stick.

"Good afternoon, sir," said Mr. Simpson as courteously as he could.

"Good afternoon. I am looking for a young woman whom I have been informed is a guest in your establishment, a Miss Alicia Cabot."

"Why yes, a Miss Alicia Cabot has been staying here, but she was married only this afternoon. She and her husband are on the fourth floor. Do you wish me to —"

His voice trailed off as the man limped to the elevator and pushed the button.

"Do you wish to register Mr. — Mr. —"

The man ignored him. He angrily pushed the elevator button again, this time with the end of his stick.

Mr. Simpson sighed wearily. This has been a very long day.

# CHAPTER TEN

# *Aftermath*

The events of the wedding day were not soon forgotten and provided grist for the gossip mill for days afterward. The euphoria of the unusual, but beautiful, ceremony in its idyllic setting continued despite the unexpected downpour of always welcome rain on the prairie, especially since it hadn't dampened spirits. But the arrival of the elderly man with the cane, which soon became common knowledge, was a spicy ingredient to the mixture of love, romance and intrigue in the opinions of the citizens of Sioux Falls who never knew what to expect from their eccentric visitors from other states.

The next morning was spent by employees of the Cataract Hotel in cleaning up the dried mud and debris which had been tracked in by guests who had raced from the dock the short distance to the hotel for sanctuary from the storm, including those who simply took refuge until it passed. The lobby was a mess and the stairs only less so, and everyone who was available was put to work with brooms and brushes and buckets, cleaning the soiled carpet before the first guests for the day would arrive. They hoped they had until at least 1:30 that afternoon, because the work was tedious and very time consuming. It was an arduous task and the maids were becoming testy at the extra workload. Some had been summoned from their day off to help out and they were not appreciative, although Mr. Simpson had assured them of "something extra" in their pay envelopes. Most of them, having known Mr. Simpson for some time, were not overly optimistic about the something extra as his extras turned out to be a pittance, and they called him a stingy miser, a double insult, behind his back. Any whispering concerning the previous day's events was promptly hushed by Mr. Simpson, who still fretted about the sad state of his lobby and the stairs, and he didn't want anything to interfere with the prompt cleanup in addition to the daily timely cleanup of the guest rooms.

Gretchen sighed and tried not to puff excessively as she and another maid, Wilhelmina, worked from the exclusive upper floor down the stairs to the lobby, finding five flights of steps to be a real chore, but grateful for a brief respite when they had to move to one side to let an impatient guest pass when the elevator proved to be too slow or too crowded. She had hoped to get some sleep after the strenuous day on the island, but it wasn't to be. She was eager to see what the something extra would be in her pay envelope. Her savings were adding up and she was pleased with that, but she would need all she could earn for the expenses of her baby. She sighed again. How nice it would be to have the extra money plus the luxury of being at home in Hartford with Nils. She really missed him. She needed him with her now and she was beginning to think she had acted in haste to have left him so abruptly. Maybe she should write that letter. What should she say? She silently composed a letter over and over again, but none of the words seemed right. However, she became convinced that it was what she should do. She couldn't hide her condition much longer. When it became obvious that she was with child she would have to leave, if she weren't discharged sooner. Mr. Simpson seemed to be breathing down her neck all the time.

"Gretchen, why don't you finish this flight and I'll start on the next one. That way we won't be in each other's way."

Wilhelmina was a fast worker and was way ahead of her and, although Gretchen was not aware of it, her friend suspected that something was bothering her, that perhaps Gretchen was not feeling well, and she decided to do what she could to ease her chores. Besides, she was also glum and uncommunicative, and Wilhelmina had hoped to get some gossip out of her, which had not been forthcoming. She didn't know that her attempts to cheer up Gretchen with her constant chatter when they were out of the hearing of Mr. Simpson had only gotten on her nerves. By the time Gretchen reached the lobby she was breathing hard and Wilhelmina was nowhere in sight. She paused to catch her breath and decided to go home and write her letter and somehow convince Nils that she really wanted to return to him and that the baby was his, although he might not believe it. She stood up and took a deep breath, preparing to take her leave. What was that peculiar smell? It was familiar, but definitely out of place in the lobby of a hotel.

"Are you finished, Mrs. Nielsen?"

She looked into the red face of Mr. Simpson, who was clearly agitated.

"Yes sir."

"Good. Then as long as you are here, you might give the other girls a hand with the rooms. There will be something extra in your pay envelope. Thank you. You are dismissed." Her heart sank. She wanted to go back to the rooming house and lie down. She was tired and getting cross. But she smiled wanly and said, "Yes sir." She was beginning to feel some animosity toward her employer. Mr. Simpson was so arrogant, yet so prissy. He talked down to "the girls." Why did he persist in calling the employees boys and girls? They were grown men and women. He made it sound so demeaning. She walked the short distance to the hall that led to the kitchen and work room to dispose of her bucket of dirty water and brushes and, when he wasn't looking, she slipped into the elevator and rode to the upper floors. She wasn't going to climb back up those steps, not that morning.

In the afternoon the hotel lobby was deserted due to the damp wool rug which gave off an odor, accentuated by another more pungent smell, so the regular guests missed the arrivals of the afternoon guests, who sniffed the air questioningly. Mr. Simpson sighed in exasperation. His trials and tribulations never ceased. He did not understand why he was so put upon when he worked so hard and performed his duties with competence and charm. Things could only improve. All the windows were open to let in the warm summer air, and the double doors on the east and south sides of the lobby also let in welcome fresh air. He presumed not to notice anything amiss and bestowed a stiff smile on each of the guests as they registered, trying to think of a reasonable excuse for the aroma that was dissipating much too slowly to suit him. But all he could summon up was, "We hope you will excuse the state of the lobby. We have had the carpet cleaned."

By evening, things were back on schedule, although still somewhat damp underfoot. Supper in the dining room was lively, with the room buzzing with conversation among the regular patrons who happily answered the questions of the new arrivals.

In the kitchen late in the evening when the maids and bellhops could finally relax after a very taxing day, they enjoyed a well-earned meal. As they lingered over their coffee, conversation was similar to that in the large dining room, but more privy to the facts. Gretchen was still there, having decided to take her meal with her co-workers rather than to trudge up 9th Street and on over to 12th to her lodgings to face questions from the boarders. She listened with interest and a very tired brain and hoped she wouldn't fall asleep. She still had to get to her room and write her letter to Nils.

Louisa was animated, as usual, and everyone listened raptly to her recital, with Billy gazing at her lovingly and tolerantly.

"Couldn't you just die?" she squealed.

The others laughed and made uncouth remarks. Gretchen stirred herself and asked, "Why, what happened?"

"Weren't you there?" asked Louisa, pink from laughter. "Oh, of course you weren't. You were on the stairs somewhere. Poor thing, what a chore. Well anyway, we got the lobby all cleaned up. It was pretty wet, but it was clean, probably cleaner than it has been for a long time, when this late arrival came in. She must have come from the Milwaukee because this fancy lady had obviously walked, because she had this large dog in tow. What kind of dog was that, do you know, Billy?"

Billy shook his head. "I never saw a dog like that in my life, all skinny with long legs and hair hanging to the ground."

Louisa giggled. "I was in the lobby just finishing up in the corner by the bank when she almost staggered in with this funny looking dog that was practically pulling her faster than she could move. She was all out of breath, but managed to keep up and the dog pulled her all the way into the lobby, then slowed down, sort of looked around, and stopped. The woman was urging him to move along, to go with her to the registration desk. But he didn't want to go—that is, he didn't want to go to the desk."

Louisa's face grew pinker with her mirth and she could hardly continue, but she clutched her stomach and made a valiant effort and said, "Well, he just refused to go one more step in spite of the woman's urging and tugging on his leash, and all at once right by the elevator by the tall brass ash container he lifted his leg and, and—"

They all got the idea and shouted with laughter, but quieted down as they saw there was more to Louisa's story.

"Well," she went on in the conspiratorial tone they loved, "he wasn't finished, you see. This fancy lady was scolding the poor dog for being 'a very bad doggie' when he proceeded to make the biggest, smelliest mess you ever saw right there in the middle of the lobby. Did you ever hear of such a disgusting thing?"

Disgusting or not, they laughed uproariously. So that was what smelled so familiar, thought Gretchen. It smelled like the farmyard they had located just outside of Hartford. No wonder Mr. Simpson was so upset. What an awful thing to happen. But she smiled in spite of it.

"I can tell you it was mighty hard to keep still, but I pretended not to notice," said Louisa.

"Go on! How could you pretend any such thing?" said one of the maids.

"Because I could see that Mr. Simpson was fit to be tied and, really, I don't blame him. That woman should have paid more attention to her dog. Who knows how far he had to travel and in a box car probably. The trip had to have been hard on the poor animal. But I have to hand it to Mr. Simpson. He kept his composure, but got awfully red in the face, and he refused to rent the woman a room, not with that dog. I can tell you she was furious. No one had ever refused her and her dog a room, not ever in all of her travels, she said with her nose in the air. Well, Mr. Simpson suggested that she try the Teton or the Merchants down the street. The Cataract was a prestigious hotel, he said, his nose in the air even higher, and it could not possibly accommodate the lady and her animal. He said 'animal' sort of funny, like he wasn't sure just what it was either. Can't you just picture it?"

"We'll be back to normal tomorrow," said Hank. "The lobby was almost dry and the smell was practically gone by suppertime. Glad I didn't have to clean it up."

"Wasn't no fun," said Mike, as the others teased.

"And what's normal around here anyway?" asked Wilhelmina.

"Oh, and did you hear about the new Mrs. McCallum's father, that Mr. Cabot?" asked Louisa. "Wasn't that something? What a way to commence a honeymoon. Billy and I were finishing up on the fourth floor. He had lots of shoes to clean after the rain and all of the guests made so many extra demands last night. Anyway, we saw this old man get off the elevator and walk right to the newlyweds' room and pounded on the door real hard with that walking stick of his. We ducked around the corner and watched."

Gretchen looked at Louisa, again appalled at her brazenness. She and Billy had actually sneaked around and spied. Still, she listened intently as she continued.

"Mr. McCallum finally opened the door. He inquired what Mr. Cabot wanted, being very surprised to find him outside the bridal suite. He didn't invite him in. That Mr. McCallum is so handsome, isn't he? He had on the most elegant satin robe with a tasseled belt." Getting impatient looks from those at the table she hurried on. "Well Mr. Cabot shouted that Mr. McCallum—he called him a young whippersnapper—knew very well what he wanted. He wanted his daughter. And Mr. McCallum said that he couldn't have her, that she belonged to him now. He said he thought they had settled this whole thing months ago. Alicia was his wife, he said, and he had a wedding certificate to prove it. Mr. Cabot raised his cane in a threatening manner and I thought he was going to really clobber that nice Mr. McCallum, and Billy had to put his hand over my mouth to keep me from making any noise."

Billy nodded. Louisa went on with her recital to her captive audience. "Mr. Cabot shouted that Alicia was his only child and he wanted her back, that he had told him months ago that he would not consent to this marriage, that his precious little girl had no future with such a scalawag, and that he took her away and brought her to this savage land of Dakota in spite of it. That's what he called it, a savage land. I don't think it's so savage, do you?"

They all shook their heads. "Well, the old gentleman continued, saying that it was no place for his innocent child, and Mr. McCallum replied that she was hardly a child anymore and that, in any event, it was too late. They were husband and wife. Mr. Cabot flew into a rage and pushed his way inside where he kept on ranting and raving and I heard Mrs. McCallum's voice, trying to calm her father down, but he wouldn't be calmed down, and we heard something break like a lamp or the water pitcher. He must have been swinging that cane of his. Then Mrs. McCallum started to cry and it was so pitiful. But that seemed to do the trick and the shouting stopped. We could hear Mr. Cabot pleading with her to come home with him and he was close to crying himself. They hadn't bothered to close the door completely, you see, or maybe they just hadn't had a chance to. 'Alicia,' he said, 'Alicia, my little princess, come home with me. I need you.' He said it over and over."

Gretchen  Billy  Louisa

"Criminy," said Hank.

"How awful for a bride. How could she make such a choice on her wedding night?" said Wilhelmina.

Why should she have to choose, thought Gretchen.

"What finally happened?"

"Mr. Cabot gave up and left—lots slower than when he got there, I can tell you," said Louisa. "Poor man, he walked to the elevator leaning on that heavy cane all humped over, his head hanging down, and I think he was really crying. He got on the elevator and Mr. McCallum shut the door and we could hear Mrs. McCallum sobbing with that nice husband of hers comforting her." She sighed at the remembrance of it.

"It was really too bad," said Billy, "no way to treat a woman."

Louisa smiled fondly at her Billy. Gretchen thought of Nils, whose behavior toward her didn't seem so bad right at that moment. She roused herself to get up and drag her weary body to the rooming house and into bed when Louisa dropped another tidbit into the rapt group at the long table, ignoring the stares of the cook and the urgings of the dishwasher to finish and move on.

"You'll never guess what Billy and I saw when we moved from our hiding place and went down to third. We took the stairs, of course."

"Of course," came a sarcastic chorus.

"Oh you—we took the stairs and paused on the landing to catch our breath."

"I'll bet you did," said Mike, grinning broadly.

"Now you stop that, all of you. I'm being very serious. Don't josh me. Billy and I glanced down the hall and there was that plain Mrs. Anderson and that good looking Mr. O'Toole kissing, kissing mind you, and it was no innocent peck on the cheek. No sir, it was one of those kisses—"

"Tell us about those kisses, Billy," shouted Hank, over the jests of the others.

Louisa had had enough of the teasing and abruptly stood up. "If that's the way you're all going to be I just won't tell you anymore."

"Aw, come on, Louisa. We didn't mean anything."

But she tossed her dark curls and she and Billy went out the back door. Billy turned, winked and waved at them good naturedly.

The lobby was filled to capacity the next afternoon. Requests for tea increased and there was much discussion among the guests, with the new arrivals taking it all in with interest. Belinda Goldworthy was ensconced in her chair trying to listen to each voice and to put down in her tablet everything she heard, scribbling as quickly as she could with her stubby fingers and hoping she got it all down correctly. She would have much to tell the Bishop after Sunday service. Mrs. Goldworthy never asked questions of any of the guests in the lobby. That would be too obvious. To ask questions would be to compromise her position.

In her quest for righting the wrongs that the lenient residency laws of the State of South Dakota had imposed upon its citizens and in her zeal and her consequent belief that no one knew what she was up to, she wrote in her tablet as unobtrusively as possible. Her large lap and enveloping skirt made it possible to appear innocent enough. Her task that afternoon was especially formidable because there were so many people talking at the same time and it was hard to follow any given conversation, but she did her best. Her cause was just and it gave her the strength she needed to carry on. She did know about the wedding on Seney Island. She had not attended it' of course, not such a pagan affair as it surely must have been, but the events of the wedding night were new to her and she caught only snatches of sentences here and there. However, properly assembled they would surely be most helpful to the Bishop.

The people in the lobby had long ago ceased to pay any attention to Mrs. Goldworthy, leading her to believe that her ruse was a complete success. Those who were accustomed to her presence knew exactly what she was doing, and her pretense of being a guest and therefore entitled to her daily afternoon cup of tea didn't fool them. The new arrivals were invariably amused by the identity of the large lady in the commodious chair and her pretense, but just as quickly lost interest, as had those who were there before them.

The Witherspoons were on the settee as usual, not saying much, but taking their tea and looking over the occupants of every seat in the lobby with interest.

"The lobby is very full today, my dear," commented Mr. Witherspoon.

"Yes. No doubt everyone is gossiping about the scandalous goings-on of the past days. And to think we attended that wedding on the island. It really makes me very upset with myself," she said vehemently.

"I quite enjoyed it. Why do you think it was wrong to go? The island was filled with well-wishers."

"With curiosity seekers, more like it," she sniffed.

"I suppose so. Still, it was nice," he replied. After a pause he added, "I haven't seen Mrs. Culpepper lately. Have you, my dear?" He looked at her with what he hoped was an innocent expression.

"Really, Waldo. I thought you knew. She left with the newlyweds. Oh don't look so surprised. And do close your mouth. It seems that Mrs. Culpepper was the new Mrs. McCallum's chaperone before she was married, that is. But you surely could have fooled me. Chaperone indeed! It comes to mind that she could have used a chaperone herself." She looked sideways at her husband. "A woman her age acting like that."

"Like what, dear?"

"Like a wanton woman," she said sternly as she looked straight at him.

Mr. Witherspoon lowered his eyes, but said in a low voice, "I thought she was rather pleasant. She danced well and she seemed to enjoy herself no matter what the occasion. Nothing wrong with that." He said it defensively.

Mrs. Witherspoon snorted. "I'm sure. And I'm sure you shall miss her, Waldo, but you'll get over it. Now snap out of it and order me another cup of tea."

Mr. O'Toole said to Mrs. Anderson, "Let's go into the dining room and have our tea. It's much too crowded out here."

Mrs. Anderson smiled and nodded. Their departure was noted without much interest, except for some of the hired help. The couple sat next to one of the curved stain glass windows on the far wall of the dining room and lowered their voices as they conversed. China cups and saucers, along with a round teapot were placed on the linen cloth and the waitress poured as Mrs. Anderson sat primly and quietly with her hands folded in her lap. Mr. O'Toole leaned back and watched her appreciatively. When the waitress had left he whispered.

"Elyse Anderson, I do love you. And you are looking particularly fetching this afternoon."

"Ted, stop it. People will start to talk."

"Nonsense. No one suspects. No one has had a clue since we arrived months ago."

"Darling, the time is dragging and there are three months left to wait before my decree is issued. You don't have to wait it out with me, you know. As soon as my divorce is final I'll come to you."

"Time spent away from you is intolerable," he replied. "Besides, I'm keeping in touch with my business in Topeka. I have good people working for me. Everything is going smoothly. In three months you will be free and we shall be married at once right here in Sioux Falls, and you shall have a very comfortable life for the rest of your days."

She basked in his words of love. The anticipation of a bright future made her eager, but she knew in all fairness that she must bring up the difficult subject of religion once more. She had to be sure she was doing the right thing.

"But dearest," she said, "you know the church won't accept your marriage to a divorced woman — a fallen woman in its eyes." Her quiet laugh was somewhat forced.

"The church will get along just fine without me. Furthermore, it will be the loser for that nonacceptance," he said firmly. "You are a good woman, a beautiful woman, and I will not hear one word against you from the church or anybody else for that matter."

At the word "beautiful" Elyse Anderson did take on a lovely glow. She was not beautiful as men define a beautiful woman, but she had a comely face, a dignified demeanor, an adequate figure, and an inner glow that emitted an aura which caused those who saw her to consider her, perhaps not beautiful, but a lady who commanded attention and respect.

"You know that I shall be branded a wicked woman who has corrupted one of the church's own, and you will be reviled along with me, Ted."

"Let them think what they will. I must confess," and he smiled ironically as he spoke the words, "that I have not been a very good Catholic in many years, my love. I was raised in the faith, but the church has not convinced me to continue in it. You and you alone have put the reality of God in my life. True love between a man and a woman cannot be wrong and I shall hear no more of this kind of talk, I have made my decision and it stands. No, no, don't cry for pity's sake."

Mrs. Anderson was indeed quietly weeping. How could she ever deserve this fine man? It was true that he had never married so she was not breaking up a marriage, but she was taking him away from his religion. It was only right that she give up her own.

She said, "Darling, I have given this much thought. You are making a great sacrifice in leaving the church. So, I shall do the same and leave mine. No, no, I mean it. However, we have to have a church. Let us choose one together. What do you think?"

He looked lovingly at her happy face and said, "What do you think about the Episcopalian?"

# CHAPTER ELEVEN

# Summertime in Dakota

It was July and it was hot and humid. A steady wind from the south provided no relief and houses and business places closed their windows early in the day in an attempt to minimize the heat. Dark green shades were pulled against the steady sun which sent scorching rays to earth where they bounced and shimmered in the moist air. There wasn't a cloud in the sky. To add to everyone's discomfort, the stench from the Big Sioux River, where raw sewage from the City of Sioux Falls was flushed, hung over the town in a suffocating fog.

"What does anyone do around here for fun?" complained Dehlia Van Tassel.

It was suppertime at the boarding house. Beulah had served the meal and retired to the kitchen with cook to eat her own meal in peace and quiet. The boarders were restless of late.

Dehlia had relived the June wedding over and over until she was shushed at last by Josephine, whose large bulk was not to be argued with when she put her foot down. The diners were attempting to keep cool as the overhead fan turned lazily, giving the semblance of a breeze. It was not the first time Dehlia had complained about the lack of something exciting to do, and the wedding was the very last exciting event that had been offered to her and that was a month ago. In the meantime, the interesting bridal couple had taken their leave, along with the plump Mrs. Culpepper, whose relationship with the couple had livened conversations when her identity became known, and now the heat and the boredom were setting in.

"I know what you mean," offered Enid Ferguson. She seemed not to mind the heat, always looking crisp and fresh even on that day when she chose to wear a high necked lace blouse. She did have her hair piled atop her head for a modicum of relief. "But I won't be here much longer. My divorce will be final in a few weeks. Next month I'll be on my way." She spoke without enthusiasm.

"We shall miss you, my dear," said Opal who refused to acknowledge any discomfort and kept to her long-sleeved, floor length dresses no matter what the temperature might be. "Where will you be going when you leave us?"

"I'm not sure. I may just return to Ohio where my family lives. I have a sister there and I do miss her and the children. But I have grown to like this city, and you have all been very gracious to me, just like family. I must make up my mind soon."

"Well you don't have much time," retorted Dehlia. "I just hope I can stand it till September when I get my divorce, before I go completely mad in this place – not you people, understand, just – this place."

"Of course, dear," murmured Mina. Her brown hair was full of tight waves and ringlets from the humidity and her face was moist from the heat.

They were lingering over their coffee which they had let get tepid, as any further intake of warmth would be intolerable. All of them were engrossed in their thoughts. Abner Faraday had dozed off and Mr. Wiggins was counting the days until Dehlia was gone. She got on his nerves to the point of making him almost speak brusquely to her. There was a limit to how much shrill talk a man could take. Somehow she had found out that his first name was Ignacious and she took perverse delight in calling him that, but in such a way as to make it sound absurd." Ignacious, would you please pass the butter?" "Ignacious, be a dear and pour me a spot more tea." Then she would give him a big smile, but her dark eyes were laughing at him. He had become her servant and one of these days he would put a stop to it. He didn't quite have the courage to stand up to her but soon now, very soon, he would put an end to her taunts. Besides, she was much too familiar with him in calling him by his first name. He should be properly addressed as Mr. Wiggins. He fervently hoped the divorcee who would take her place at the table would be a nice, refined young woman with whom he could carry on a decent conversation. His conversational skills were minimal, at best, but he was confident that all he needed was the right woman to bring out the essence of what constituted Ignacious Wiggins.

"Where are Louisa and Gretchen?" inquired Enid.

"Those poor girls are all tired out. There has been a lot of extra work at the hotel due to an unprecedented rush of

97

new arrivals daily and, consequently, they aren't back yet," said Mina. "We'll hold supper for them because they will be hungry. Gretchen looks rather peaked, but she hasn't lost any weight. I hope she is all right. She must be expecting a letter, because ever since she wrote a long letter to Mr. Nielsen she has been somewhat anxious for a reply – at least it seems so to me."

Josephine looked at her sister and spoke sharply. "Just how do you know all this, Mina? Surely, you have not been poking your nose into Gretchen's business. You are just too curious for your own good."

"No, Josie," sniffed Mina, "I haven't been poking my nose where it doesn't belong. I only saw her leave in the direction of the post office. She had asked if we had any stamps to mail a letter to Hartford, so I just assumed –"

"Our guests are entitled to privacy, Mina. You must remember that."

Josephine hated being called Josie and she knew when Mina called her that she was putting her in her place for having chastised her in front of their guests. It must be the oppressive heat that was making everyone cross in their discomfort. She pushed straggles of white hair back into the coil of her braid and looked around the table to see the diners leaning back in their chairs, enjoying the repartee between the two ladies at the end. Josphine cleared her throat and changed the subject.

"Now then, Miss Van Tassel, to answer your question, there is plenty to do in Sioux Falls even in the summer. I might add, especially in the summer. There is boating, of course. We have a brand new Carnegie Library on 10th Street not far from here. We are extremely fortunate that Mr. Andrew Carnegie saw fit to give the city a library of such magnificence. And there are recitals of various kinds in the auditorium on the second floor of City Hall. It seats 3,000, you know, and there is the annual Chautauqua held in the auditorium for literary readings, including poetry, and for plays. We have splendid stores and shops and –" She could see that her words were having little effect on the bored Dehlia who was stiffling a yawn.

Dehlia continued her recitation of complaints. "Why aren't women allowed on the golf links around here anyway, I get so tired of whist, and checkers are a real bore." Then she brightened and added, "I almost forgot; I heard some dandy gossip just today down on Main Avenue."

The sisters bristled and wished they had risen to signify that supper was over, but it was too late. Abner Faraday stirred himself and muttered, "Eh? What?" Dehlia gave him a playful wave of her jeweled hand and teased, "I knew that would make you pay attention, Abner, old man." Abner never knew that she loved to tease him as well as Mr. Wiggins; he just enjoyed watching her, especially her decolletage, so he smiled a toothless grin back at her.

"Well this is what I found out; I heard that a Mrs. Lord who has that Temple Court down on Main got brought down a peg or two when her wild son was run out of town."

Enid gasped and covered her mouth with her lace handkerchief. "That' s right, run right out of town, and you want to know why?" She didn't wait for an answer, just laughed her ear splitting laugh and said, "It seems he was having some fun with some very young girls in his apartment there, and I mean young, not out of their teens yet. Can you beat it? He was plying them with spirits and who knows what else. Naughty boy." And she shrieked again and slapped the table, making her water glass jiggle and almost tip over.

"Really, Miss Van Tassel," said Opal as she and her sisters rose from their chairs, "I think that is quite enough. In these very lax times one hears so many disturbing stories. I choose not to put any credence in what you have said." She pushed her gray hair back into her bun, adjusted her steamed over spectacles, and left the table, gathering as many supper dishes as she could. She bustled busily about in her consternation, realizing that her comment on "lax times" was a direct insult to the ladies at the table, but she was hot and irritable. It had just popped out. The Van Tassel woman was enough to try one's patience. Josephine and Mina followed her into the kitchen, laden with dishes, surprising Beulah.

"Honestly," commented Josephine, "sometimes I wonder if we are doing the right thing in offering sustenance and solace to those poor souls seeking a divorce. Are we not being hypocritical in doing so?"

"Don't get overheated," replied Mina. "It's just this awful weather. Everything will look differently when it cools off. If it would just rain."

"I think I'll play a hymn tonight to sort of smooth things over, sort of make things right. Don't you think so? Don't you think a hymn would help to sort of calm things? A hymn doesn't necessarily have to be limited to a Sunday now, does it?"

"A good idea. Play something soothing and settling," said Josephine.

The boarders were seated on the south porch trying to catch the waning wind, which seemed to stop as soon as the sun began to set. Some rocked in the wicker chairs, some sat quietly. Abner Faraday was dozing, but woke with a start when the peal of the organ under Opals heavy foot was heard. "Lead Kindly Light" rang out with the voices of the three sisters singing in harmony on every one of the many verses. The sound filled the big house and spilled outside into the stillness of approaching dusk. There followed "Bringing in the Sheaves" as the sun sank to the horizon in a brilliant red ball, taking its time as it hovered on the landscape. The last chord was struck as dusk fell on the silent group and a slight breeze sprang up.

The heat continued with only sporadic rainfall which was quickly absorbed in the prairie dust. It was August. Enid Ferguson got her divorce and departed for Ohio, promising to return someday for a visit with her newly made friends. The citizens of Sioux Falls grew restless as the dog days of summer progressed slowly and tempers and behavior reacted accordingly.

In front of the Cataract Hotel the people of the city were accustomed to seeing a pitiful man seated on a flat cart on wheels low to the ground. The man had no legs below his knees. They had been blown off during the ill-fated entry into the Spanish American War by the First South Dakota Volunteer Infantry Regiment. The man had made his go-cart himself and he propelled it along at a goodly speed with gloved hands. He was a bootblack earning a living by shining and repairing shoes. He did good work and had many repeat customers. He had a rough appearance with untidy chin whiskers and he smelled bad. The ladies avoided him, never looked at him, trying to pretend he wasn't there, but it proved difficult, because he always lifted his dirty cap in an obsequious manner when one passed by, knowing it upset them. Most ladies learned to steer clear of the east entrance to the hotel during the day. Men accepted him because he posed no threat and he gave a good shoe shine. Shorty, as they called him, always had the latest news, the juiciest gossip, and he loved to impart it piecemeal as he tended to his patrons' shoes.

He was not allowed inside the Cataract, but he bothered

no one and was tolerated until sundown when he had to take his departure. The unspoken agreement worked for both Shorty and Mr. Simpson, who also denied any knowledge about the poor man on the cart outside the hotel. He would inform any inquisitive guest that the bellhops would gladly collect any shoes or boots that were left outside the guest's door each night, guaranteeing that in the morning they would be found intact, repaired and shined to a fine polish. But any really curious guest would stop and engage Shorty in conversation while getting an inexpensive shoe shine.

"Thank ya, sir. Come agin," he would say with a grimy, toothless grin as he tipped his soiled cap. To more than one gentleman he would look up beneath shaggy gray brows, wink and ask, "How do ya enjoy them rooms in there, sir?" He would jerk his head at the hotel behind him.

One portly man replied, "Splendid, just splendid. This hotel is as good or better than some in the East and I've been in my share of hotels."

"I hear tell there are some wicked going-ons in thar at times." A chuckle from Shorty made the man inquire what he meant.

"Well, I heard there's some dandy poker parties inside there till the wee hours. That so?"

"I couldn't tell you, I just arrived yesterday. I do play poker though; it helps pass the time."

"I heard of one of those poker games that really passed the time," Shorty smirked.

The gentleman's curiosity was certainly aroused and his other shoe was still to be shined, so he asked, "What do you mean, my good man?"

"Well ya see, this here one was raided. Seems it was strip poker they was playin' and Mr. Simpson found out about it. You know Mr. Simpson. He don't cotton to any such going-ons in his 'stablishment. Mighty fussy man, Mr. Simpson."

"Strip poker. You mean —"

"Yep, and there was some high falutin' lawyers doing the strippin'. Heard tell there was some ladies present, too, but don't know much about that part." Shorty said "ladies" with another smirk, and was gratified to see that he had properly shocked his customer.

"Good heavens! I never heard of such a thing, not in a place like this," remarked the man.

"Times is changin'. Morals is loosenin' up. Seems like anythin' goes nowadays, don't it? By the way, let me know if ya want to know where to go to have a good time. Thank ya, sir," he said with a broad wink as the man flipped him a coin and walked on, shaking his head.

"Shorty, you old dog, you sure get your jollies by shocking gentlefolk, don't you?" Bart Kelly placed his foot on the shoe dummy as he taunted the old man. Bart was a regular customer and had a good time talking to the scurrilous man, oftentimes obtaining some gossip to pass on.

Shorty gave a nasty laugh and said, "Yep, I like to shake up those fancy, uppity folks, bring' em down a peg. Besides, I never pass on what I can't back up." He raised his shifty eyes to see if Bart was inclined to believe him.

"Sure you do, Shorty. Any good bits for me today?"

Shorty paused in his occupation with buffing Bart's not so soiled shoes, taking his time, knowing he was in no hurry. "I believe I do now I think on it. Been mighty hot, ain't it?" Again the shifty look upward.

"Hot isn't the word. Are the summers up here always like this?"

"Long as I bin here, and that's a spell. Yep, been mighty hot. Some folks go a mite crazy with the heat, I hear tell." He saw that he had his customer's attention. "Yep, they sure go crazy." He buffed deliberately, waiting for a response.

"Shorty, you old coot, out with it. What happened? Did someone go crazed from the heat?"

"Might say so, I reckon. Peculiar anyways. Seems like some of the looser ladies in town decided to cool off a bit." He began to chuckle so hard he could hardly keep on buffing and his low platform was starting to wobble.

"Come on, you dirty old man, tell me."

"Well, I was scootin' along the other day, mindin' my own business down there on the west side of Phillips, when I spied a crowd gathered all along the whole block, mostly menfolk, and they was shoutin' like they was at a fight or somethin'. I scooted across the street and saw plenty, havin' such a good ringside seat here," and he patted his low cart as he snorted. The menfolks was a'hollarin' and a'yellin' and all at once I seen these bare legs go runnin' past, female legs, mind you. There was two ladies—" he said "ladies" with derision, "naked as the day they was borned, havin' a foot race to see who could git to a bottle of beer at the end of the block." Remembering the

102

sight Shorty doubled over in obscene laughter.

Bart was intrigued with the old man's tale and urged him on, "What did they look like and who won?"

"What does any female look like naked, man? I didn't look at their faces, but their hair was sure flyin' around. By the time the race was over they was clawin' at each other and pulling hair to get that beer. Lawd; What a sight. 'Nuff to keep me happy all winter."

Bart flipped him a coin and walked on. How could he have missed that performance? He'd have to spend more time in town and forego the dog fights for awhile.

Shorty was still chuckling and talking to himself. "Don't know if that frakus cooled 'em off none."

Shorty often had to have help in getting home. He had friends, from shady characters in his neighborhood on the East Side to the bellhops from the Cataract. He liked to stop at a tavern on 8th Street before he rolled on home and many a night he would never have made it across the bridge without assistance. One particularly hot night toward the end of August, as he was helped home by some of the bellhops and they got him into his shack and into his filthy bed, he stirred when the nature of their talk seeped into his sodden brain.

One of the hops was saying, "Yeah, some of the men are asking where to go for some fun, what there is to do for some entertainment."

Billy was not usually one of those who helped Shorty to get home, because he thought him most unsavory, but for some reason, he was on that night. He agreed and said, "It's mostly the men. The ladies always manage to keep busy. They have more patience. Did you ever notice that? How much patience the ladies have?"

"Billy, you are so innocent. Don't you know what those guys want?" asked Mike.

"Sure I do, but even Mr. Witherspoon, of all people, has asked me and how do I answer him? You know I could never tell him about that place, not that nice old man. But he keeps saying that he's writing a book about Indians and he's here to do some research, only there is a problem. He's never seen an Indian."

"Tha's some problem, ain't it?" slurred Shorty. "You bin readin' them western magazines, boy?" He pulled himself up and said, "Well now, I know where those gents can have some fun, a real good time, and even fin' a Indian." Shorty smiled and peered up at them with bleary eyes. "Do it have to be a brave?"

The young men were interested. Shorty knew everything. He had their full attention. Billy squirmed and wished he hadn't come.

"Now this here is what we kin do," said Shorty, grinning his toothless grin, slobber running into his whiskers.

*The falls of the Big Sioux River. (Photo courtesy of the S.D. State Historical Society)*

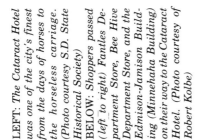

LEFT: The Cataract Hotel was one of the city's finest from the days of horses to the horseless carriage. (Photo courtesy S.D. State Historical Society)

BELOW: Shoppers passed (left to right) Fantles Department Store, Bee Hive Department Store, and the Edmison-Jamison Building (Minnehaha Building) on their way to the Cataract Hotel. (Photo courtesy of Robert Kolbe)

ABOVE: *The Minnehaha Building (Edmison-Jamison Building in this volume) in Sioux Falls.*

RIGHT: *The Queen Bee Mill used the power of the Big Sioux River to start one of Sioux Falls' most important early enterprises.*

ABOVE: *Sioux Falls' first hospital. (Photo courtesy of Robert Kolbe)*
LEFT: *Minnehaha County Courthouse was architect Wallace Dow's masterpiece. (Photo courtesy of the S.D. State Historical Society)*

110

*Turn-of-the-century Victorian homes. (Photo courtesy of the S.D. State Historical Society)*

LEFT: *Dickinson's Confectionary and Bakery. (Photo courtesy of Robert Kolbe)*
BELOW: *A winter day on Ninth Street. (Photo courtesy of Robert Kolbe)*

# CHAPTER TWELVE

# The Mansion

Billy didn't want to go through with it. The whole thing went against his grain. And he sure wouldn't tell Louisa. But the arrangements had been made and he had the distasteful task of hiring a hack and making sure it did not arrive at the hotel too soon and was out of sight in the alley. He was relieved that he hadn't been assigned the job of notifying all the "gents" of the plan. He wouldn't have done it anyway. Hank got that one and he didn't seem to mind. In fact, his sidekick, Mike, was more than glad to help him out. How they could go about such a delicate assignment Billy had no idea, nor did he want to know. He wished he could get out of the unpleasant business, but his manly pride prevented him from making any objections.

So he sent a letter to a Mr. Towter, stating that he would like to hire transportation for 10 or 12 men at a late hour on the next Tuesday. Shorty told Billy that this Mr. Towter would know what he meant. Billy suggested a meeting in the alley behind the Cataract when the day help had gone home and it was pretty quiet.

He was in the alley, hating himself, and wishing it was over when he heard a clattering heading in his direction. He soon made out the form of a man astride a very large black horse. He pulled up just out of Billy's line of vision and inquired if he would be the person by the name of Billy Stone. Billy swallowed hard and said that he was. The man identified himself as Mr. Towter and said he could provide any kind of transportation on the next Tuesday, depending on the number of gents needing to be transported, for the price of $2.00 per gent, for which he would transport them and return them to the hotel. What they had to pay once they reached their destination he couldn't say. Billy told the man there would be 13 in all, a number he privately considered to be extremely unlucky, given the circumstances. Mr. Towter said he would return on Tuesday night at 11:30 on the dot. If his passengers weren't all ready to go or were not there he would leave, taking it as a sign they had changed their minds. He then wheeled his horse around and clattered noisily back down the alley. To Billy's ears it sounded loud enough to raise the dead and he looked nervously around to see if anyone had come out the back door to see what all the racket was about. But no one did.

He reluctantly relayed the man's message to Hank and Mike who smiled broadly and departed at once to deliver the terms to the men involved. Billy was shocked to learn that Hank, and Mike were among the thirteen.

"Aw, come on, Billy boy, don't be an old lady. Why don't you come on along?"

He looked at them in disgust and walked away.

The remaining days of August continued hot and humid, but the skies were increasingly overcast, giving some relief from an unrelenting sun. On Tuesday there was no afternoon sun and no breeze. The heavy atmosphere was filled with an imminent storm, making folks edgy. There was no sundown, only deepening dusk, and it was very dark before 11:30 arrived that night.

Louisa was late in seating herself at the table in the kitchen that evening and Billy was thankful for that. He had earnestly implored the others to not mention the upcoming late night activities and, for Pete's sake, to not mention his part in it. They all agreed and as the maids looked on in disdain the bellhops whispered hoarsely among themselves, but ceased abruptly as Louisa bustled in, her black curls bobbing. She noticed nothing out of the ordinary in her preoccupation with her haste.

"Sorry to be so late, but Mrs. Clayborne just wouldn't be satisfied tonight—must be this miserable weather. She wanted clean towels, then she needed her high topped shoes polished and new laces added,and you know how long that takes. She didn't want any of you fellows to touch her shoes, only me," she said with a teasing glance, and she was puzzled by the lack of rejoinder. Ordinarily, she would have been assailed with loud remarks regarding Mrs. Clayborne's lack of appreciation for the expertise of the many bellhops who shined countless shoes every night of the week.

"Well anyway, it took longer than I thought and when I

was finished she took them without so much as a thank you. That woman is such a snob. I'm glad I'm not one of her personal maids. She expects so much from them. They have to practically read her mind as they follow her everywhere in that suite, because if she intends to walk into another room the door had better be open, because she doesn't slow down one whit, and a chair had better be where she wants to sit, because she says nothing, and if they weren't quick enough she would land flat on the floor. How does she manage that?" There was no response. "What's the matter with all of you? Are you mad at me? Is my cap on crooked? What?"

Louisa's cap was usually on crooked by the evening, so no one noticed or commented. The hops only smiled sheepishly, not daring to look at her. The maids excused themselves as they removed their soiled aprons and tossed them in the laundry chute, said good night to Louisa, and left without saying another word. Louisa said in exasperation, "I'm too tired and hungry to bother with you. What's good tonight, Billy?"

Billy was glad to change the subject and said, "You're in luck. There's still some ham, and dessert is chocolate cake."

"Wonderful," and she sank into her chair as Billy gladly went to fetch a plate of supper for her.

The bellhops left, leaving the lovebirds to themselves, and the pressure lifted from Billy. Louisa eagerly ate her supper, chattering away, as he sat back and tried to act nonchalant. His part in the conspiracy was over. He only wanted to get out of the hotel and see Louisa home before the wagon arrived. It would surely make her ask questions and demand answers.

"Goodness, it's really close, isn't it?" she said, as she dabbed at the perspiration on her forehead. "There's not a breath of air. All the rooms upstairs have the windows open as far as they will go, but it doesn't help much. And it's so pitch dark out tonight. Maybe it will finally rain and cool off."

Billy sincerely hoped so and that it would soak the men to the skin. But the rain took its time in coming. Deep rumblings could be heard across the clouds which looked strangely misty gray against the pitch black sky. Now and then a sheet of lightning lit up the sky, illuminating clouds that were swiftly gathering, clouds with puffy bottoms, making them look like they were upside down.

"Just heat lightning," said one of the hops to the men assembled in the alley behind the hotel. The kitchen was dark and the arc light at the end of the alley on 9th Street cast an eerie glow which didn't quite reach the group of 13 men, young and not so young, who had gathered around a wagon pulled by a team of husky horses. In the wagon seat, holding the reins in gloved hands, sat Mr. Towter all dressed in black with a large black hat which covered his features. He was not recognizeable, and he didn't intend to be. He made no comment on the ribald remarks of his customers as they climbed aboard his wagon, handing him their $2.00 as they did so. They had to be satisfied with sitting on the floor of the wagon, which made an uncomfortable ride, but they didn't mind. The team lurched forward at Mr. Towter's command, accompanied by a crack from his whip which snapped menacingly just above their rumps.

Hank and Mike grinned at each other and passed around a bottle of whiskey that someone had brought, with each man taking a swig. Most were on their way to being slightly inebriated, making their discomfort on the floor of the wagon less noticeable.

The Willow Dale Mansion was one of several brothels outside the limits of the City of Sioux Falls. It enjoyed its greatest patronage in the 1880s and 1890s and had achieved such a reputation that it became a source of outrage to the upstanding citizens of the city, all of whose railings against it had gone for nought. It continued to operate into the 1900s. It was located outside the city limits on West 12th Street on the west side of the river that wound around Sioux Falls. Its idyllic setting was in sharp contrast to the boisterous goings-on in the sturdy wood building which was set close to the water, surrounded by elms and cypress trees.

On August 29, 1889, the Argus Leader editorialized:

"There is one thriving business in Sioux Falls, at least, and that is what is called 'Willow Dale Mansion' or in other words Madame Doyle's bagnio west of town. Hacks go through the western part of the city at all times of the day and night filled with drunken men and boys. It is becoming such a nuisance that property owners are beginning to get desperate."

Those who frequented the place ignored the sharp reproof and business continued as usual. The mansion operated openly and without restraint. Being outside the city limits protected it—but no Sunday picnics were held in the vicinity.

The team avoided the downtown area and clip-clopped to 12th Street where the momentum increased once the wagon had left the residential area. Mr. Towter ignored the drunken songs which began to emanate from behind him. He didn't care and he knew it made no difference as long as he made such a comfortable, easy living in his sordid livelyhood. He and Shorty had done well for themselves, splitting the profits, although there were times when Shorty came out on the short end, but he never tumbled to it, because when Mr. Towter paid him when Shorty was drunk, he also shortchanged him without Shorty's knowing the difference. Mr. Towter had put away thousands of dollars during his career and had built a reputation as being a knowledgeable, dependable man who could see to the needs of the local men in a more or less discreet manner. So far there had been no trouble.

Hank and Mike grinned at Mr. Witherspoon seated in a corner of the wagon. It was clear that he was excited, even though he was not really drunk, having not been in the habit of drinking, mostly as a result of being married to Mrs. Witherspoon. They had promised to take him to see an Indian, a real live Indian, along with some other gentlemen. Mr. Witherspoon had a pad of paper and two sharpened pencils to take notes. What luck. He would finally get some first hand information and begin to write in earnest on his book about Dakota. His research had to be accurate and what would be better than an interview with one of the natives? He didn't quite understand, though, why they had to travel so late at night, and where on earth were they going? Perhaps to an Indian settlement. He had heard there were some Sioux natives somewhere nearby, some graves on the west side of the city, and he thought they were traveling due west, but it was so dark that he couldn't really tell.

As he observed the other men drinking so heavily he felt a twinge of apprehension. He had heard what happened when liquor was passed around to Indians. These men were setting a bad example. He had to admit that he had taken a sip when the bottle was passed around and he was feeling pretty good, making his creative juices flow, but he surely didn't make a habit of sneaking around. Those young bellhops, Hank and Mike, were very nice to bring him along even though it cost him $2.00. They had told him he shouldn't mention it to the missus, because she probably wouldn't understand why he had to go out at such a late hour. Mr. Witherspoon didn't understand that part either, but he had become very bored with his life and it was so hot and the whole outing sounded like an exciting adventure. Mrs. Culpepper was gone and he missed her. She had been such fun. He wished Mrs. Witherspoon would loosen up a little and have some fun now and then.

"Are we almost there" he asked.

"Yeah, it's just over the bridge a little ways yet," Hank replied. The hops snickered.

At last the wagon turned south on a bumpy dirt road. It followed the river a short distance and in the trees by the water was the Willow Dale Mansion. A high stone base protected the wood building from any rising water. There were several small windows on all sides of the building through which smoky light filtered. Loud music and raucous laughter could be heard. The wagon pulled up to the front door which had a lit red lantern on each side gleaming fuzzily in the gathering haze. The river beyond lay like a lead sheet with no reflection almost like ice solid enough to walk across. The stillness rang with sounds of revelry coming from the square building. The smell of strong, cheap perfume, cigar smoke, and other assorted odors assailed the nostrils of the men as a full-bosomed middle-aged woman opened the door.

" 'Evenin' gents," she said. "Come on in. Enjoy yourselves." She smiled brightly with a heavily rouged mouth.

Mr. Towter said to Mike, "I'll be back around 1:30 o'clock to haul you all back," and he flicked his whip over the backs of the team of horses and continued south to some unseen exit. Mike waved him on as he stumbled behind the others into the brothel.

The room was large and decorated with gaudy, baroque furniture. Risque pictures hung on the walls. The windows were covered with heavy, velvet draperies, predominately red, provoking a feeling of anticipation and excitement. Painted women in various stages of undress evoked wild hoots from their new customers who went off with some of the girls on carpeted stairs to an upper floor. Some of the men decided they needed a drink first and were served whatever they wanted by other scantily clad females who made their own choices, sitting on the arms of the plush chairs or on the men's laps.

Mike said to the woman who had opened the door, "This here fella wants to see an Indian," and he winked a knowing wink.

The madame smiled her crimson smile and her mascaraed eyes looked into the questioning eyes of a trembling Mr. Witherspoon. "Why sure, we can take care of him. What's your name, honey?"

Mr. Witherspoon, quite taken aback since his entry into the bawdy house, realized where he was and he knew he had been hoodwinked. He stammered, "Witherspoon, Waldo Witherspoon."

"Well, Waldo honey, you come along with me. I have just what you're lookin' for."

"No, no, I think not. I've changed my mind. You see, I thought we were going to an Indian village. This is not at all what I had in mind."

He was resisting her, protesting, as she took him firmly by the arm and guided him to a corner. "Come on now. Don't be shy. You won't be sorry. We can find an Indian for you. There, see? Here's one now."

She beckoned to a young woman who emerged from a shadowy corner into the light and Mr. Witherspoon's mouth fell open. She was dressed like an Indian, at least from the pictures and drawings he had seen, but her skin was far too fair to be an Indian. Her hair was black and it hung in a braid over her breasts which were scarcely contained in the laced bodice of her short dress which barely covered her knees with its long fringe, which moved provocatively as she moved toward him. A beaded head band with a red feather encircled her head. She glided to him, looking up at him with blue eyes.

"I'm afraid there's been a mistake," Mr. Witherspoon cried in a frightened voice as he was pulled toward the stairs. "I only wanted to talk to an Indian, that's all—preferably a brave."

The girl just smiled and urged him up the stairs. "Come with me. Let's see how brave you are."

Hank and Mike were in stitches. Madame Doyle spoke, "Seems like a real nice man. Joyce will be good to him." Whereupon the hops were convulsed in laughter until two girls took them away to what they hoped would be their wildest dreams come true.

Around 1:15 in the morning Mr. Towter and the team were waiting at the front door facing in the direction of 12th Street when the revelers straggled outside and clambered into the wagon. They were much too somber and subdued for having experienced what they had come for.

"Where are the rest?" he inquired behind him.

"Oh God," moaned one of the older men.

Just then Hank and Mike, totally sober and scared, came through the door and the lights went out immediately at the door.

"What's this?" demanded Mr. Towter in a gruff voice, annoyed at having anything out of the ordinary transpire in what should be a smooth operation. Without any lights the already opaque darkness was impenetrable. The lamp hanging on the front of the wagon was swinging perilously in a brisk wind.

"We've got a dead man. Get us back to the hotel real quick," said someone.

"What?! Damn! I didn't bargain for this. What happened, was there a killing?" He asked it as though it happened now and then.

"No, looks like a heart attack."

"Good God, not that. That's even worse. Where is he?"

Mike's face was ashen in a flash of lightning. The wind was strong and the air was cool, but it was full of unvented fury that was sure to break soon. The unsettled change of weather was making the group jittery. The horses snorted and stamped the ground impatiently.

Mike spoke. "Me and Hank's got him. We'll have to pile him in the wagon. We need some help here. He's not so big, but he's dead weight and it's quite a lift."

Unwilling hands reached over the side of the wagon as Mr. Witherspoon was lifted up to be placed on the bottom of the wagon where his limp, lifeless body seemed to accuse them all. The rest of the men lined against the sides of the wagon as far away from the deceased as possible, trying not to look at him.

"Isn't there anything we can cover him with?" asked a man.

"This guy's too old to be out here anyway. Ten to one he's never been to one of these places," said Mr. Towter angrily. He turned to glare at them. "This is going to cost you all extra."

No one spoke. They sat slumped in the wagon, wishing with all their hearts that they were someplace else. The wind blew dry leaves and swirls of dust around the wagon. Streaks of lightning jabbed the dark sky. Thunder echoed loudly and it was evident that a storm would break soon and that all due speed was needed in getting back to the hotel. Mike and Hank were sullen. How could things have gone so wrong? Mr.

Witherspoon had been so pathetically eager, and so comically bewildered. They were only having a little fun, for Pete's sake. What would they do once they got back to the hotel? What would Billy say when he found out? What would he do to them when maybe Louisa found out? What about Mr. Simpson? They were doomed.

The horses leaped ahead at the crack of the whip and broke into the best gallop they could given the terrain and the load they pulled. Large drops of rain made dust puddles in the road. They turned onto 12th Street and headed east as fast as the horses could go. The drops turned to heavy sprinkles, then to sheets of rain, and to torrents that burst from the dark, noisy sky. Within seconds they were drenched to the skin. There was nothing to cover poor Mr. Witherspoon with and his face grew pasty white as the rain pounded him mercilessly. Mr. Towter swore fiercely. The men covered their heads the best they could and pondered their fates as the horses jostled the wagon and its miserable cargo back to the city.

# CHAPTER THIRTEEN

# Farewell to the Witherspoons

Mr. Towter took a slight detour from the steady jog east on 12th Street and turned down Minnesota Avenue to 19th Street, stopping a short distance from the rear entrance to the Sioux Falls Hospital. The rain continued to pelt the men in the wagon. He turned to the huddled group, scowled menacingly beneath his broad brimmed black hat, and spoke tersely between clenched teeth, as rain dripped from the brim.

"Now this is what you will do. Get this old man to the door and ring the outside bell. Then get back in the wagon as fast as you can, because I'm not going to wait for you. Get going!"

Four of them got out of the wagon with dead Mr. Witherspoon and gently laid him beneath the overhang of the outside door where a dim, flickering light shone. Three of them scrambled back aboard the wagon which began to move, as the fourth man rang the emergency bell and raced after the departing wagon. There was no sign of anyone or anything by the time the door was opened by a sleepy and very surprised nurse when the body was discovered.

There was no sound except for the wind blowing blankets of rain over the city and the rapid hoofbeats of the horses pulling the creaking wagon. No one spoke, but it was clear that they were exonerated. There was nothing to connect any of them with Mr. Witherspoon's untimely demise and it was unspoken that none of the men would say a word, and they didn't have to worry about Mr. Towter saying anything, except for his anger, which seemed to hang over them all like their own personal storm cloud. They were deposited in the alley behind the Cataract and Mr. Towter took his leave after collecting an additional dollar from each of them. No one argued about it and they hurried into the hotel as the whip cracked once more and the horses took off at a gallop now that they were relieved of their cargo, as their master let forth a stream of profanity that dispersed in the falling rain. The alley was quiet once more, with no one the wiser.

In the early morning hours around 5:00 o'clock some of the guests were awakened by a scream that mounted in crescendo as the news of Mr. Witherspoon's death was relayed to Mrs. Witherspoon by Dr. Edward Evans from the Sioux Falls Hospital. Mrs. Witherspoon was sitting upright in bed in her rumpled nightdress, her hair disheveled, staring at the empty side of the bed where her husband was supposed to be, where she last saw him. A tired maid stood at the door, wringing her hands.

"Waldo?" Mrs. Witherspoon said in disbelief. "But he was here. You must be mistaken," she protested, as she looked into the kind doctor's eyes, searching for confirmation.

"I am so sorry to disturb you at this hour, with such sad news, Mrs. Witherspoon, but I felt you should be told at once."

"But he was right here." She touched his pillow where a slight indentation could be seen.

The good doctor realized that his self-imposed task of informing this woman of her husband's fate would be more difficult than he thought. He tried again.

"Mrs. Witherspoon, I know nothing more than what was told to me by the night attendant at the hospital. I was on duty last night and had just finished late rounds when the nurse rushed in and said she had answered the emergency bell and found a man lying just outside the door. No one else was there, only the deceased."

At the word "deceased" Mrs. Witherspoon set up a wail that could be heard on the entire floor. Dr. Evans moved to the bed, sat beside her, and tried to comfort the distraught woman. He patted her shoulder and took her hands in his and said as soothingly as he could, "Please Mrs. Witherspoon, I assure you that your husband didn't suffer. Death came quickly."

She looked at him in disbelief. "No. No, you're wrong. He was right here. You must have him confused with someone else." She closed her mouth in a grim line as though to say that the matter was closed.

Dr. Evans persisted. "We found his wallet with his identification in it; it appeared that no money was stolen. I take it there are no children, no relatives to notify"

"We didn't have any children," she answered unhappily and covered her face with her hands.

"Oh yes, we found something else in his wallet. They look like penciled notes of some kind. They are hard to decipher, having gotten wet from the rain, I suppose, but we could make out the word'Indian' here and there."

Mrs. Witherspoon moaned softly and swooned into her pillow.

News of the death spread rapidly in the hotel and, gradually, into the general population and the presumed knowledge of Mr. Witherspoon's demise was spread as well. However, the guests at the hotel kept that news from reaching the widow's ears and tender sensibilities. In any event, she would not have believed it. The bellhops and those male guests who had accompanied them on their ill-fated adventure were subdued, which others took to be an attitude of respect. The maids knew better, though, and their displeasure and outrage could scarcely be concealed. Mr. Simpson was beside himself. Such a thing had never happened to a guest of the Cataract Hotel. As if he didn't have enough to do – now he must deal with the awkwardness of an unexpected and untimely death. His distress did not extend to curiosity as to the circumstances, only as to how it would affect the reputation of the hotel and his own reputation as well. Any interest he had was satisfied by his brief interrogation of Hank later that morning. Mike and Hank figured they had better show up for work as usual to allay any suspicion that might endanger their jobs. They had to keep their part in the happenings of the previous night a secret. There was no sleep to be had upon their return anyway. They had huddled in the store room where they dried off and decided on what to say if either of them happened to be questioned. They donned their uniforms, had their breakfast with lots of coffee, and tried to act surprised when the news got out.

"Yeah," Hank said to Mr. Simpson, who had stopped him and asked if he had heard about Mr. Witherspoon, the elderly gentleman who had been with them for several months. "I hear tell it was his heart." His head was bowed. He added, as if in some kind of personal vindication, "He was pretty old."

"A heart attack? Curious. And just why was he out on a night like last night? The Witherspoons never venture out

124

late at night. What on earth were they doing?" He looked at Hank with his piercing eyes, his red lips pursed in question, demanding an answer.

"I dunno, Mr. Simpson," he stammered, squirming. "The way I hear it, the missus wasn't with him. They found him at the hospital door." He stopped abruptly, thinking he might have said too much.

But Mr. Simpson didn't pursue it. "Strange. Very well, you are dismissed. I am sure you have work to do."

"Yes sir." Hank gladly made his escape. His encounter with his employer had to be the worst one he would have. He should be able to handle any others. He wondered how Mike was faring.

Bart Kelly, being more savvy to affairs of the world, had his suspicions regarding the sudden death in the middle of the night of an old man out in a raging storm, but decided to keep them to himself. No sense in spreading rumors and upsetting the grieving widow, to say nothing of his own credibility and reputation. If he was where Bart thought he had been it was no wonder he had a heart attack. Poor old fellow. He never did write his Indian story. Bart suppressed a wicked chuckle. Oh, Lord, he thought, you don't suppose Madame Doyle supplied him with an Indian. He raised the afternoon paper over his face as a snort escaped from him and he was in danger of exploding into a guffaw. It wasn't funny and, yet, considering who the victim was, to Bart Kelly's unscrupulous nature it was a matter of considerable amusement. He pondered the various stages of seduction Mr. Witherspoon must have been subjected to before he succumbed to whatever throes of passion he was capable of. The newspaper began to quiver alarmingly.

There was no one to take charge, to help Mrs. Witherspoon, so kindly Dr. Evans took it upon himself to look after her until the funeral was over. His death certificate indicated that death was due to a heart attack, which Mrs. Witherspoon accepted. Perhaps it was the only thing she could accept, because if she had any idea of why he had left the marriage bed and ventured out into the wild night and why he had been discovered at the emergency door of the hospital, she gave no indication.

The L. D. Miller Livery Barn stood on the corner of 11th and Main close to downtown Sioux Falls, with the L. D. Miller Funeral Building next door. Two doors down was Ballard & Sons Monuments, a tidy arrangement making it convenient for the grieving to take care of arrangements with a minimum of effort. The body of Waldo F. Witherspoon was transported to the funeral home by one of their coaches. He was laid out in his best Sunday suit for a few hours before he would be laid to rest. There were no out of town relatives to wait for and the steamy weather made a speedy interment mandatory. Mrs. Witherspoon entered the funeral home on the arm of Dr. Evans and wept silently by the casket as he stood a few steps behind her. At last he took her arm and she turned to find the room full of people who had come to pay their respects. She was surprised to see so many. Dr. Evans led her to a chair and they filed by her, greeting her cordially, telling her how much they had enjoyed knowing her husband and of how he would be missed. She thanked each one for their attendance, and wondered how she could not have known that her Waldo had made so many friends. Some of the remaining residents with whom she had become acquainted and who were still at the hotel were there; maids and bellhops told her they liked talking to her nice husband. Mr. Simpson came and stayed briefly, for the sake of appearance; but Hank and Mike begged off, claiming extra duties at the hotel. In fact, they had volunteered for those duties to avoid having to go through the torture of seeing Mr. Witherspoon again and reviving the guilt they shared in his demise.

Most of the people in the room left to attend to their own business, but some continued to the renamed Calvary Episcopal Church on 13th and Main for the funeral. The Witherspoons had attended church every Sunday, as regular as clockwork, but now Mrs. Witherspoon was alone and seated in the front row for her Waldo's funeral. It all seemed so unreal. The Episcopal Church was only a short distance from the funeral home, located on a pleasant grassy rise. The service was to be conducted by Bishop William Hobart Hare, founder of the church and a leader in the rigorous battle to lengthen the residency laws required to obtain a divorce in the State of South Dakota.

Mrs. Goldworthy was in attendance, seated in the pew which she claimed as her own in the second row. She nodded to Mrs. Witherspoon who smiled, remembering Waldo's comments on the stalwart Mrs. Goldworthy when he would remark to his wife that the woman never took her copious notes on a Sunday, whereupon Mrs. Witherspoon would only look at him in disapproval as he smiled at her with a wide grin, knowing she could not argue with him in church. She missed him terribly already. The reality of his death was sinking in. Could she have taken him for granted all the years they had been married? He was so patient with her.

A lovely soprano voice sang "Nearer, My God, to Thee" and she felt her eyes fill with tears and brim over. The regret welled up inside her, but it was too late now. She and Waldo could have enjoyed many more years together. They had wasted far too much time doing nothing in wild South Dakota. She should have encouraged him to write the book he was always talking about instead of waiting for him to forget about it. A pang in her heart reminded her that the only real fun he seemed to have was with that chubby Mrs. Culpepper, who meant no harm. What a bitter lesson to learn, too late. The hymn ended and the singer sat down. Bishop Hare approached the lectern and looked with compassion at Mrs. Witherspoon and began to speak. His sermon was brief, but inspirational. He noted Mr. Witherspoon's devotion to his God, his church and his wife. He was a good man, whom the community would sorely miss. Then it was over and she was led to a carriage by Dr. Evans for the trip to the cemetery.

The procession of carriages, preceded by the black funeral coach drawn by two handsomely adorned black horses, made its way slowly. The driver was somberly dressed in black, complete with a black top hat. Mrs. Witherspoon sat dociley beside Dr. Evans, seemingly detached from what was happening. Despite the intense heat she sat pale, withdrawn and silent, cloaked in a long-sleeved black dress. A black bonnet with a small veil sat squarely atop her head secured by a taffeta bow tied beneath her chin. The procession was short as many of the visitors had returned to the hotel.

It was a small number of mourners who finally turned into the entrance of Mt. Pleasant Cemetery. Mt. Pleasant Cemetery was the first cemetery in the City of Sioux Falls. Established in 1873, it was located about two miles east on 12th Street, the edge of the city. The carriages traversed a stony trail that wound upward around grave stones of various sizes set amid evergreen trees that were growing tall against the bright blue sky and puffy clouds. Some of the monuments to the dead who were buried long ago were old, dating from the Civil War. Made of pink and of white sandstone, they were beginning to tilt slightly from age and the inscriptions were not as legible as they once were. They proceeded to the rear of the cemetery where a mausoleum stood, stark on a rise at the south end, with the name SAGE, 1889, engraved above the door. She shivered. This whole thing was so final. They turned again and came to a stop, facing north where she could see the entrance. Among the stones were heavy urns, some of which were ornate, decorated with cherubs and birds. The plants and flowers they contained drooped with the heat.

She felt the doctor's hand on her arm and she stirred herself for one last ceremony. She stepped from the carriage and said a faint, "Oh," as she saw the open grave. Strong men positioned the casket containing her Waldo over it and she drew back against Dr. Evans. He put his arm around her small shoulders and led her gently to the commital site. The eyes of the few remaining people who had accompanied her were on her. Dr. Evans didn't let go and his support was all that sustained her. Bishop Hare stood at the head of the grave, resplendent in his robe, holding a Bible. When she had steadied herself he intoned a blessing over the casket, said a prayer for his soul, and committed Waldo F. Witherspoon to the earth and into the hands of God. Mrs. Witherspoon felt faint and was not able to move as the doctor tried to turn her away from the sight of the casket being lowered into the grave, while two sweaty men in their shirtsleeves waited patiently with their shovels.

"Come, Mrs. Witherspoon, it's all over," she heard as she was led back to the carriage. Her vacant eyes took in nothing as she was transported back to the hotel and Dr. Evans saw her up to her room, which was now solely her own. He sat her in a chair and she didn't move, didn't remove her hat, didn't speak. The good doctor's job was finished, but he was loathe to leave the bereft old woman. However, it was imperative that he return to the hospital. He bent over her and took her gloved hands. They were oddly cool to the touch.

"If you need me, just send someone for me, or give me a ring on the telephone."

She gave no response. He sighed, bid her good-bye and shut the door quietly behind him. In the lobby he left instructions with Mr. Simpson, who did not seem interested in what he had to say, which was that if Mrs. Witherspoon needed anything, he was to call him at the hospital. As he left the hotel he muttered under his breath, "What a pompous little man." Mr, Simpson fiddled with the keys and messages in their cubbyholes, giving the task his full attention.

Within a week Mrs. Witherspoon had left the Cataract Hotel and returned to her home in Ohio, leaving so quietly and unobtrusively that she was not noticed. In no time at all the Witherspoons were forgotten, as though they had never been there.

# CHAPTER FOURTEEN

# Chance Meetings

August melted into September with little letup in the oppressive heat.

"How many months of summer are there in this awful place" complained Dehlia Van Tassell, Even with her low cut dress and bare arms she was warm and she patted her pale skin with a colorful handkerchief and wiped her brow where her auburn curls clung in tight ringlets. Abner Faraday watched in appreciation. They were seated on the porch of the boarding house, trying to catch a cool breeze after supper. The sisters were on the porch around the corner, giving their guests some privacy and enjoying some of their own. They rocked slowly, the wicker creaking in protest, as the sisters idly fanned their flushed faces with palm-shaped fans they had recovered from an old trunk.

"Where are Gretchen and Louisa?" asked Opal in a tired voice. It was hard to be a gracious hostess when one was so uncomfortable and one's guests were getting somewhat testy in their own discomfort.

"I believe they went upstairs, but I would think it would be cooler out here," replied Mina. Josephine closed her eyes, leaned her head back into a pillow, and rocked, fanning her face.

Upstairs on the third floor Gretchen lay on her soft bed; her tight shoes had been tugged off, and she lay with her arms outflung, exhausted. A knock on her door made her groan inwardly, but she said politely, "Yes, who is it?"

"It's Louisa; may I come in?"

Gretchen rolled to the side of the bed and got up, She didn't want to see anybody. She was hot and cross and wanted to go home. But she got up and opened the door and smiled a welcome to Louisa, who had become a good friend.

"Louisa, come in. My, isn't it hot?"

"I'll say. Did I disturb you, Gretchen?" She noticed the

rumpled spread. "I don't want to be a bother."

"No, I was just lying down for awhile. It's too early to go to bed, not that anyone could sleep in this heat."

Louisa stood uncertainly inside the door and Gretchen looked at her with curiosity as she closed it. Her friend's lust for life was gone and the animation Louisa usually exhibited was strangely absent.

"Let's sit over by the window. It might cool off soon and maybe a nice breeze will come up as the sun goes down." She said it without much conviction.

They sat in roomy arm chairs by the big window that looked east to the downtown area where a haze hung over the city. The lace curtains were pulled back as far as they would go. They hung limply and did not stir. Gretchen wiped her damp throat.

"I don't remember it being this hot on the farm, especially this late in the year."

"Do you miss it?" inquired Louisa, by way of a start in the conversation.

"Yes I do, very much," Gretchen said quickly and with more fervor than she had intended. Her eyes filled with tears and she turned her head away.

"Gosh, I'm sorry, Gretchen. Didn't mean to make you cry."

Louisa's own eyes brimmed and the two women dabbed at their moist faces, sniffled and blew their noses. They looked at each other, smiled in sympathy, and then laughed. Louisa spoke.

"This is so funny. I came up here to cry on your shoulder and here we are, two grown women, bawling our eyes out and neither of us knows exactly why."

Gretchen felt a surge of relief and said, "Louisa, I have to talk to you. You are a good friend and will understand. There's no one else who will. I'm at my wit's end and don't know what to do. I – I don't know quite how to explain."

Louisa looked at her with compassion. "You're going to have a baby, aren't you?"

Gretchen was incredulous. "Why yes. But how did you know? I've told no one. Is it that obvious?" She smoothed her skirt over her round abdomen.

"Well, yes, it is. And we've all commented on your, well your healthier appearance. When you came you were so thin, and now – oh, your poor swollen feet."

Gretchen raised her feet and viewed them with disgust. "I can hardly get my shoes on anymore and I'm on my feet all day long, I guess my apron doesn't hide my condition much," She let her feet fall down and rested her forehead on her hands. "Oh Louisa, what am I to do? I've written to Nils telling him I want to come home, but he hasn't answered me."

"Does he know about the baby?"

"No, I just couldn't tell him that in a letter."

"Are you sure it's —?"

"Oh yes, it's Nils's baby. I could never —. But when I left him I had no idea I was in a family way or I would never have left."

"How I envy you. You have a home and a husband — and I'm sure he'll come around — and a baby on the way, all the things I ever wanted, and now, I just don't know."

"But you have Billy. He's such a nice young man. We all assumed you two would be married soon."

"So did I, but now I'm not so sure."

"What made you change your mind? He is so in love with you; we can all see that."

"Don't you know what he did?,

"Why no. What did he do?"

"You remember that poor Mr. Witherspoon, the nice old man who died that stormy night?"

"Yes, he was always so pleasant. He and his wife were sort of permanent fixtures at the hotel. She seemed rather domineering, though."

"Well," said Louisa, with a bit of her former spark, "he died of a heart attack all right, but do you know where he had that heart attack? I'll tell you where. He died at that dreadful whorehouse, the brothel west of town, you know — The Mansion,"

Gretchen gasped in disbelief.

"No, not Mr. Witherspoon. He would never go out there. He couldn't."

"Ah, but he did," said Louisa, warming to her outrage. "It was all arranged for him to go with a wagonload of men from the hotel, including some bellhops, who shall not be mentioned in this conversation." She tossed her head. "But the part that is so hard to take is that Billy was the one who made the arrangements to take the men out to that place."

"Oh Louisa, no. Why?"

"He said he couldn't get out of it. His manliness was at

stake, some such silly reason. Everybody tried to keep it from me and I feel like such a fool, the only one in service who didn't know, and Billy pretending all this time."

"He didn't go, did he?"

"He says he didn't and I do believe that, because he had to work that night, and I know for a fact that he did. But to think that he had a part in that poor man's death, well it's just too much to bear, and it's so unlike him, Gretchen."

The tears turned to sobs and Louisa's fire was quenched as she buried her head in her hands.

"My goodness," said Gretchen as she got up and went to her. "You mustn't feel like that. Billy had no way of knowing any such thing would happen, and I'm sure it was not the first bunch of men from the hotel who have gone to The Mansion. Come now, don't cry, and don't blame Billy. You love him and he loves you. Don't throw that away. You know how men are. They have to feel so – so manly." She said it with her own expression of disdain and she started to cry.

The two women clung together and sobbed out their anger and frustration, finally quieting and comforting each other. They dried their puffy eyes and gazed at the other's disheveled appearance, at the limp hair clinging to their perspiration-dampened foreheads, their wrinkled clothes and tear-stained cheeks. Sympathetic smiles turned to giggles. Finally, Gretchen spoke.

"This is really funny. I came to Sioux Falls to find a job and earn a lot of money to be independent of Nils. I figured if I had to work as hard as I did as his wife I was going to be paid for it. Now I am growing big with child; exhausted from the work I do; much of my money goes for expenses, plus expenses I'll need for the baby: and I'm lonesome for Nills and my home. It's all been for nothing."

Louisa said between giggles, "And I thought that since I was worked to death at the Cataract by our beloved employer, if I had to work that hard I would prefer to be married and do it in my own home with my Billy. And now that seems impossible. Isn't this ironic?"

The strange turn their lives had taken did seem absurdly funny and their emotions turned giggles into laughter. The sounds of their laughter carried out the third floor window to the boarders and the sisters rocking on the porch.

"I guess the ladies are upstairs after all. It's hard to imagine what they found to laugh about. It has to be very hot up there," said Mina.

Soon thereafter, a cool front brought a breeze from the north, gentle cleansing rains, and a lifting of spirits. Tempers calmed, rumpled nerves smoothed out, the air freshened and the wind blew the stench from the Big Sioux River away from the city.

The time came for Dehlia Van Tassel to get her divorce and she was more loud and shrill than usual as the date fast approached. She was beginning to wear on the boarders and the sisters and they were all secretly glad to soon be rid of her. No one had yet arrived to take the place of Enid Ferguson; there would be two rooms for the sisters to fill as well as two places at the table. Their bank account had grown to a comfortable sum, but as with any good fortune, the larger it grew, the larger they wished it to be.

Dehlia had determined to make a grand appearance in court and set out to buy herself a new wardrobe one sunny afternoon in early September. The sisters sincerely hoped it would be of a more conservative nature. She had been, by far, their most flamboyant boarder and they had talked of screening their future guests more closely. Abner Faraday would miss her, as she was loud and gaudy enough to command his attention and he enjoyed her teasing. Ignacious Wiggins was counting the days till her departure.

She began at Fantles, purchasing a fall suit, a form filling dark green skirt which flared just above her new high-topped button shoes. The jacket fit as snugly, fastened tightly at her small waist and flaring in a peplum, slightly longer in the back. The collar and cuffs were trimmed in white fur. She was assured it was genuine ermine, which she chose to believe. The hats didn't suit her so she instructed the salesgirl to have her purchases delivered to her boarding house and continued to The Hat Shop where she took her time and reveled in the close attention paid to her by salesgirls eager to sell the goods that were priced to the limit for purchase by the many divorcees, whom they had learned to fawn over.

The Sioux Falls Hat Shop was an exclusive shop on Phillips Avenue that catered to the expensive tastes of a clientele who could well afford it. Hats of every description, made of the finest materials, adorned with plumes, feathers, birds, flowers and satin bows could satisfy even the most finicky woman. Hats were on display and also stored in large drawers which lined the walls of the small shop. The drawers were of a walnut finish, giving off an elegant patina of refinement. Mirrors mounted on top of the drawers reflected a pleasant ambiance. Walnut cupboards were topped with plants and ferns. Accessories of ribbons, pins, gloves and purses were displayed in glass cases. An air of quiet good taste pervaded the room, which subdued Dehlia to the point of civility, lowering her usually loud voice to a more normal tone as she was approached by a salesgirl.

"May I be of assistance, Madame?"

Dehlia rose to the occasion and said levelly, "Yes, I am in need of a nice hat to accompany my new suit."

"And what is Madame's color preference?"

"Green; my suit is dark green with ermine trim." She stated this with an arrogant flair.

"Of course, Madame. I am sure we have just the thing. Follow me please."

Dehlia glanced around her as she followed the salesgirl to a display of hats with various trims of fur. She could see a stylish older woman seated before a large mirror, commanding the attentions of a salesgirl who had been sufficiently cowed into submission and who was desperately trying to please her. Dehlia kept an eye on them in a mirror as she tried on several hats, having already found precisely what she wanted, but not wanting to consummate her purchase right away. She heard the woman say,

"No, no. That's not it at all. This hat is much too large. Haven't you this style in something with a smaller brim?"

She frowned impatiently. The girl continued her search through a drawer while the woman preened and turned her head as she donned one hat after another, each one looking just fine in Dehlia's mind. She must be that hoity-toity woman from the Cataract, the one the gossips had linked with some lawyer fellow. She eavesdropped as she tried on the hats again, pretending to have difficulty in making up her mind.

"Perhaps this is more what you have in mind, Mrs. Clayborne."

So it was her. She was a regal looking woman whose attitude was indeed imperious, but to Dehlia's mind she only just put on airs. Dehlia knew airs when she saw them, but since she was in such a posh shop she decided to try some airs herself. She took her pretense one step further and ventured to volunteer her opinion when a particularly attractive hat was produced and placed on top of Mrs. Clayborne's shining coiffure.

She said, "Pardon my intrusion, Madame, but that one is perfect, in my estimation, just perfect with your hair and coloring." She smiled and was pleased to see that her ruse had worked. Mrs. Clayborne gave her a weak, slightly haughty smile in return.

"Why thank you. I have had a dreadful time making up my mind. Do you really think this one is right?" she asked as she turned her head to see every angle in the mirror.

"Oh yes. It brings out the color of your eyes. Most attractive, don't you think?" she inquired of the salesgirl, not realizing that it was not proper to speak with such familiarity to an employee. The girl replied softly, averting her eyes, "Yes Mum," and fit the dark blue hat slightly to one side of Mrs. Clayborne's head and fixed it to her heavy hair with a hat pin embossed with shiny stones. A moderate plum-colored plume wound around the medium brim. Mrs. Clayborne gazed at her reflection with satisfaction, barely looked at the weary salesgirl and said shortly, "This one will do. Please apply it to my account and have it delivered to my suite at the Cataract."

"Yes Madame," she said as she scurried through the scattered hats, grateful that her ordeal was finished.

Dehlia turned back to making her own selection and was able to see Mrs, Clayborne looking at her and then approaching her.

"Thank you for helping me make up my mind. I have been so out of sorts lately that decisions have become burdensome. My name is Clare Clayborne."

"Dehlia Van Tassel. Glad to offer an opinion, but I didn't wish to offend."

"You didn't. I haven't seen you in the shop before."

"As many months as I've been in this town this is the first time I've been in here. Have to look my best when I go to court tomorrow."

"You are here for the purpose of obtaining a divorce, too?" asked Clare in an unaccustomed exchange with a stranger.

"Yeah. I mean, yes. It seems more like six years than six months. Actually, it's been more than six months. My residency was up last month, but my lawyer couldn't get it scheduled until tomorrow. Still, it's quicker and lots easier than in New York."

On impulse, Clare asked, "My dear, would you care to join

me in a cup of coffee; that is, if you have made your selection?"

"Sure. I mean, yes, I would really enjoy that. This one will do," she said as she handed a green hat with white fur trim to the salesgirl with as much aplomb as Mrs. Clayborne had. She paid for the hat and said she would take her purchase with her. She didn't want her highbrow companion to know that she lived in a boarding house.

The ladies decided to go to Dickenson Bakery & Confectionary between 10th and 11th Streets on the west side of Main Avenue. "Dad Dickenson's Cafe" as it was called was a popular place for divorcees to eat or to gather for conversation. R. W. Dickenson, with his unusual attire, was one of the sights for out-of-town visitors. His hair hung to his shoulders and he wore a long white coat which reached his high boots, giving him the appearance of a kindly grandfather. He had come from England in 1888 and established his bakery in a building which resembled a small castle, complete with a tower. Windows in the upper floors set in the middle of the building allowed ample light, but kept the appearance of a medieval structure, It was built of jasper stone, enhancing the illusion. Dad Dickenson was a generous and warm hearted man and enjoyed a profitable business, catering to the citizens of his adopted home and to its burgeoning population of divorcees who gave it a continental atmosphere.

On their brief walk to the cafe Clare Clayborne pondered her impulsiveness in speaking to the stranger at her side and to inviting her to partake of some refreshment. Maybe it was the welcome change in the weather, making for greater sociability. Maybe it was because she was very lonesome. Maybe it was because this Dehlia person had made the right choice about the hat; she had good taste. Clare decided not to worry about it but just to enjoy the lovely afternoon. They took their time, not wishing to get too winded from the incline to Main Avenue.

"Whatever possessed the founding fathers of this city to plan it on all these hills?" she asked as she began to puff in spite of herself.

"Something to do with building along a river, I guess," replied Dehlia, surprising them both with her unexpected logic.

They were soon on Main Avenue and at the door of Dickenson's and paused to catch their breaths before they made their entrance. All the women made an entrance at Dad Dickenson's Cafe, knowing it was always full of curious customers. It was expected and provided much of the attraction to the cafe. Those seated always faced the door. Clare preceeded her and Dehlia took note of the grand lady's manner and modified her more showy entrance accordingly. She was having a good time, hobnobbing with a rich woman of some breeding and she wasn't going to spoil it. They were rewarded with admiring stares and murmured comments as they were seated at a table in full view of the rest. After they were served their coffee and chocolate eclairs, which they had convinced themselves they had earned after their strenuous afternoon and the climb up the hill, they took a sip of their coffee laced with cream, and relaxed.

"Well, that was a lark," quipped Dehlia, as she crossed her legs, then quickly uncrossed them at a disapproving look from Clare.

"Tell me, my dear, how is a divorce accomplished? I fear I must wait until November, and it would help to know what to expect."

"Well," responded Dehlia, "Alphie says that it will be very simple and will take no time at all. We simply go into the judge's chambers, tell him my grounds for divorce, and after presenting the necessary papers the judge signs the decree and I walk out a free woman, after paying my lawyer, of course."

"That is basically what I've been told, but is it true that the courtroom won't be full of curiosity seekers, people who have no business being there?"

"That's right, because it's a closed court, you see; that is, if you don't go into the judge's chambers where it is all very private. Alphie said that no spectators are allowed. It's just you, your lawyer and the judge. Simple, huh?" She took a bite of her lucious eclair, licking her fingers. She quickly wiped them on her napkin and dabbed at her mouth, catching Clare's disapproving look. But that is not what was bothering her companion.

"Pardon me, but did you say Alphie? Is that your lawyer's name?"

"Yeah. I mean yes. It's short for Alphonse. Did you ever hear of a more dopey name? I mean, who would name a child Alphonse?" She was enjoying her eclair and sipped her coffee appreciatively. "This is really good, isn't it? Say, you haven't touched yours."

"This Alphonse, his last name wouldn't be Grafton, would it?" Clare asked with an effort.

"Why sure it is. Good old Alphie. He's very good at divorces, and he's taken real good care of me while I've been here. I've talked to other women who have him for their lawyer and they swear by him. Some swear at him, too, I hear." And she gave a meaningful look at Clare as she chewed her last morsel of eclair.

"What on earth do you mean?"

"Well honey, I mean, Mrs. Clayborne, he's a rake. The old fool thinks he is irresistible to women and he'll try anything to get all he can out of them, more than just a hefty fee, if you understand what I am implying."

Clare understood all too well. She turned pale, then flushed with embarrassment. She quickly raised her cup to her lips hoping Dehlia had not noticed. But she had.

"You don't mean it. You have Alphie, too? Well what do you know about that. Say, he hasn't tried anything funny with you, has he? You know, some of that malarky about his wife not feeling well. Heck, she's healthy as a horse and about as big as one, too. Have you ever seen her?"

Dehlia gave a laugh that caused heads to turn. She patted Clare's arm.

"Take it from me, Mrs. Clayborne. Alphie is a good lawyer, but keep him at arm's length. Get your money's worth, but don't allow him any liberties. Take it from someone who knows what she's talking about. Say, aren't you going to eat your eclair?"

Clare pushed it toward her and rose, leaving coins on the table.

"You'll have to excuse me, Mrs. Van Tassel. Thank you for your company."

What a dreadful mistake she had made in letting down her guard and being in the company of someone so lowbrow as Dehlia Van Tassel. She conveniently overlooked the fact that her lowbrow companion had given her pertinent information that she should take to heart. She left the cafe with dignity, holding herself stiffly erect, sweeping through the door as a gentleman opened it with a bow just in time.

# CHAPTER FIFTEEN

# *Happy Endings for Some*

One afternoon a short time after Gretchen's and Louisa's heart to heart talk, Opal answered a knock at the front door of the boarding house with anticipation, hoping to find someone looking for a good place to stay for a few months, and stepped back in wary surprise at seeing Nils Nielsen standing there, hat in hand.

"Hello Ma'am, I'd like to speak to Gretchen, if you please," he said politely. His face bore a solemn expression.

He appeared calm enough so Opal relaxed and said, "Of course. Come in and I'll get her. She's up in her room. Please wait in the parlor." She waved her hand in the direction of the parlor where a previous angry confrontation had occurred. She hoped this visit would be more civilized.

Upon learning that Nils was waiting for her, Gretchen's face brightened with joy as she ran to the stairs. She hurried to the parlor, then slowed and with hesitation entered the room, closing the door gently behind her.

"Nils," she said softly. He stood at a window staring through the long curtains shaded by the heavy tasseled drapes. His hat was in his clasped hands behind his back. She noticed that he was wearing his good suit and his hair was neatly trimmed. He turned when he heard her voice, looked long and hard at her, then the hat dropped from his hands and he held out his arms. She rushed into them.

"Nils, oh Nils, you're here," she sobbed with her face buried in his chest. He smelled of strong soap and Bay Rum.

He held her closely to him and breathed in her scent. They clung together for a moment, their hearts pounding, and then he abruptly held her at arm's length and stared. There was more to her, a softness and a roundness that was new to him.

"What's this?" he asked.

Her eyes were streaming and her cheeks were wet. She

could scarcely see him as the tears coursed down her tired face. She blurted the words while she had the courage.

"I am with child. The baby is yours, Nils. It's our baby. I didn't know when I left or I never would have done it. I never should have left you in the first place. I know that now. Please, Nils, I want to come home. I love you dearly and I need you and I want to be with you. I want to raise our baby and live out my life with you in Hartford. Will you take me back? Can you ever forgive me?"

She could not have been more contrite, The poignant look on her face and her heartfelt sincerity touched Nils's heart. His thoughts reeled with the unexpected news he had just heard. He had been prepared to be very stern, to not give in easily, but to take her back. Her letter pleading with him to be reunited was most welcome, but his manly pride would not let him reply immediately. He had been bewildered and deeply hurt by her rash action and she had to know that. Even through his anger to find her gone ran the knowledge of his constant love and the conviction that Gretchen belonged to him and no one else. His uncompromising attitude melted away and he took her in his arms tenderly and whispered,

"Get your things. We have a lot to talk about on our way home."

She was crying with happiness and relief as she ran from the room and up the stairs as fast as she could, considering her condition. In no time she reappeared with her suitcase and purse, wearing the clothes she had worn when she arrived at the door of the sisters. Admittedly, there was a more snug fit than when she arrived, but she managed to get the skirt on, leaving the top buttons undone. On hearing her crying and her rush upstairs, the sisters were waiting for her as she reached the bottom of the steps, slightly out of breath, and they knew at a glance what had happened from the joy emanating from the faces of Mr. and Mrs. Nils Nielsen. They beamed in response to their happiness.

Josephine spoke, standing tall and in charge. "Gretchen, my dear, I take it you are leaving us?"

Gretchen's smile made her look years younger with the traces of fatigue and worry erased. "Yes, Nils is taking me home. Isn't it wonderful?" She gave her husband a loving look, then said, "I am so sorry to not give you any notice, but I only just now found out myself and I have to leave. I hope you will forgive me."

"Of course, we do understand," said Opal with a stab of envy at the very real affection between the couple. "We have enjoyed having you as our guest."

Mina impulsively gave her a hug. "I am delighted for you, Gretchen. We wish you every happiness."

"Thank you. You have all been so kind to me and I have appreciated it more than you can know. Please tell the gentlemen good-bye for me. I'll write to Louisa."

Nils picked up her suitcase, turned to the sisters, nodded politely, and donned his hat. He held the door for Gretchen and she waved to the ladies standing primly in a row as they said their farewells, and she and Nils walked down the steps for the last time.

The sisters stood together with their hands clasped before them and sighed in unison. Gretchen had been the ideal guest, but now she was gone and there were three rooms to fill. But the dismay at their decreasing income turned to their usual dignified civility as two young women approached. They looked with curiosity at the happy man and woman descending the porch steps as they climbed upward to inquire about rates for room and board at the large house on the corner of West 12th Street.

Nils had brought the horse and buggy. It was a nice day, the roads were dry and passable, and they had much to talk about. He figured that on the way home to Hartford would be as good a time as any to do just that. They headed west to the edge of town, turned north with the sun beaming gently down and a cool breeze fanning their faces. His strong hands held the reins with authority and Gretchen felt warm and secure in his presence, and she wondered how on earth she could have given it all up. How she had missed him. She could admit that now as she looked at him with love and affection, admiring his strong profile. She could also admit that her brief adventure into independence had not been for nought. She had learned some of the ways of the world and knew it could never be her world. The big city had taught her to fully appreciate the good people in Hartford. She had taken too many good things for granted. She knew now where her roots were and where her baby's roots would also be. Nils had a serene smile on his face and he was savoring the news that he was to be a father. Gretchen knew gratitude in his acceptance, without question, of the fact. She knew satisfaction, too, in having earned a sum of money that was sure to come in handy when the baby arrived.

They didn't speak for a mile or two. Soon the City of Sioux Falls was behind them. Its noise and smells disappeared, supplemented by the sweet scent of the sunlit countryside which was filled with ripening grain. She breathed deeply and watched the birds as they swirled above them high in the sky, singing with abandon.

Nils finally spoke, without looking at her. "I missed you, you know. And — and I do love you." He glanced sideways at her.

She slid over to him and he put his arm around her. Gretchen was a happy woman. She smiled to herself. She never did match her curtain material.

Divorces continued unabated by the controversy in the City of Sioux Falls, despite the opposition of the churches and the Women's Christian Temperance Union. The Catholic Church did not recognize divorce and therefore no divorcees were permitted to partake of the church's rituals. Bishop Marty of the Catholic Cathedral of St. Michael was adamant in his refusal and turned his energies and attentions to the Indians in the area, offering not only the wherewithal to food and shelter, but the opportunity for the redemption of the souls of the "savages."

Bishop William Hobart Hare of the Calvary Episcopal Church likewise would not permit divorcees to participate in church functions, and likewise was noted for his missionary work with Indians. Both men were leaders in deploring the degredation the divorce mill, or the divorce mecca, as it was also called, had brought to the Queen City of the Plains.

So when Mrs. Anderson and Mr. O'Toole had decided upon a compromise in choosing a church, that church being the Calvary Episcopal Church, they appeared before the Bishop. They stated their intentions and also requested that he marry them when Mrs. Anderson's divorce was final in a few weeks. They were dismayed to learn of his displeasure and outright refusal to do either. Humiliated and disillusioned, they left the city and the State of South Dakota as soon as they could, boarded the Great Northern to Omaha and were speedily married in Nebraska. They enjoyed a brief honeymoon before traveling on to Mr. O'Toole's home in Kansas, where they lived happily and in comfort from his profitable business.

Judge Bruno Addison was a busy man. He had been granting divorces for ten years and he had earned a tidy sum for his old age, plus a fountain of material for his memoirs when he retired. He insisted on twenty minutes to a half hour between cases to make sure that all papers were in order and to prepare himself for the next one. His cases were for a variety of causes, from a man's complaint about his wife's refusal to take a bath, causing revulsion in his sleeping with her, to a woman's complaint that her husband's many women friends were spoken about to her as his "orchestra" and of one in particular as his "first violin" causing the wife to feel distinctly out of tune. Such nonsense. But the city had seen its share of celebrities and the final disposition of their complaints was in the Courthouse on the corner of Sixth Street and Main Avenue.

The judges' confabs over drinks at the end of the day were filled with gossip and riotous mirth at the shenanigans of those who came before them demanding satisfaction and the righting of wrongs, real or imagined. In the early days of the divorce colony James G. Blaine, an American statesman from the State of Maine, was divorced by his two wives in Sioux Falls. Judge Addison smiled in remembrance of it. It was in the early years of his practice when he was abashed by the prominence of the people who came before him. He soon overcame his awe and accepted as a matter of course the various causes of action presented to him, with clients being represented by any one of a multitude of lawyers the city had spawned. By September the number of divorces granted approached 100.

Several options were available to men and women seeking a divorce, contested or uncontested, If they arrived in the City of Sioux Falls to begin their six months stay to establish a residency and if the divorce was contested, the aggrieved plaintiff could have suit commenced in Canton, a small town in Lincoln County, some 25 miles southeast of Sioux Falls. When the Sheriff of Lincoln County could not locate the defendant, he returned the papers to the plaintiff's lawyer, who then mailed them to a lawyer in the defendant's home town in whatever state for him to institute service to accomplish the job.

Sometimes a previous arrangement would be worked out between the parties. The plaintiff would arrive in Sioux Falls, establish residency and retain a Sioux Falls lawyer to appear for her. The defendant would previously arrange for another lawyer in the city to represent him and appear for him, along with a supportive deposition to sustain the plaintiff's complaint.

Many opted for sticking out the 180 days plus the weeks

it took for papers to be served and answered to obtain a divorce.

Dehlia Van Tassel was one of those who chose that option for reasons not clear, even to herself. Whatever the reason, whether mere ignorance of the options open to her or the fact that she had plenty of time and managed to make the most of any situation the designated time for her court appearance came. She made a flashy appearance decked out in her newly purchased outfit which displayed her fine figure. She clung to the arm of Alphonse Grafton, who beamed his pleasure. He enjoyed being in the company of any presentable, attractive woman who had money, even one as strident as Dehlia Van Tassel.

In the space of a few minutes Mr. Grafton made his usual impassioned exhortation to Judge Addison concerning his client, who had been sorely wronged by her scalawag of a husband. His client's conduct was pure and unsullied and she could no longer tolerate his unreasonable, bestial behavior. Her only recourse was to seek a dissolution of the marriage through the auspices of the court. And on and on went Attorney Grafton. Judge Addison could recite his soliloquy by heart, as could his clerk who sat at a table beneath his lofty seat. He looked long and hard at Dehlia as she sat languidly in the dock, her long legs crossed, displaying a trim ankle. The judge had a twinkle in his eyes and she gave him a wicked wink, as Mr. Grafton droned on. Finally, Judge Addison heard him come to a close, he turned serious and intoned, "Divorce granted," and signed the decree.

Dehlia jumped from the dock in glee, grabbed Mr. Grafton around the neck and planted a loud kiss square on his lips, complained about his mustache tickling her, then whooped,

"Come on, Alphie, let's celebrate"

Mr. Grafton made the obligatory objections for appearances sake before the judge, stammered all the reasons for its not being such a good idea, thoroughly entertaining Judge Addison and his clerk with his embarrassment. But she insisted, proclaiming that he would not get paid until they had a little celebration.

As they left the courtroom arm in arm, leaving the room echoing with Dehlia's shrill laughter, the judge and his clerk could hardly keep from bursting into undignified hoots. Judge Addison chuckled at the sight of the barrister's red face and crimson neck as he was led by his unbridled client, oblivious

# CHAPTER SIXTEEN

# *Autumn*

Louisa was seated on the squeaky porch swing at the boarding house. She had received a letter from Gretchen and could hardly wait until Billy joined her so she could read it to him. She was also filled with excitement at what she would say to him. She had no doubt that he would agree wholeheartedly.

It was a lovely evening in mid-October when the weather in South Dakota was at its best with warm sunny days and refreshing breezes and cool nights without the frigid nip that would soon arrive, causing one's breath to vaporize. The fresh, brisk air was invigorating, motivating body and spirit to action. Thoughts of the coming winter when the ever-present wind turned icy and blew sleet and snow into drifts which clogged the streets were far from people's minds. The perfect weather was to be enjoyed while it lasted.

Darkness fell early and Louisa slipped on a shawl as she waited, swinging gently. Light shone warmly from the living room window behind her. Louisa was content. At last she heard his footsteps and his familiar "Hey, Louisa sweetheart, your Billy-boy's here," as he climbed the steps.

She laughed and shushed him lest the sisters make some sign of disapproval. Billy leaned over her and gave her a kiss. He wanted to take her in his arms in a big bear hug and cover her with kisses, but knew he would be summarily chased off the porch by the sisters when they would hear the alarming squeaks that would then emanate from the resultant movement of the swing, to say nothing of the peals of laughter from the two lovers.

"What's up?" he inquired.

"Oh, Billy, I got the nicest letter from Gretchen today and it made me feel so good that I just had to read it to you, and then I have something to say to you."

"OK, shoot." He leaned against the porch railing.

"She says,

'Dear Louisa,

Just a note to let you know that everything has worked out wonderfully for me and Nils. He is absolutely thrilled about the baby which is due in December. Maybe it will be a Christmas baby! Boy or girl, we don't care. We've waited so long that it doesn't matter. I am so excited, and to know that Nils is, too, makes my happiness almost more than I can bear.

It has all made me want to urge you once more to forgive Billy, to take him back, marry him and have your own baby. Nothing is more important than that. You will never regret it.

Nils and I hope that you and Billy will come to see us, perhaps next summer. Hartford is not like Sioux Falls, but I think you'll like it. By next summer Nils has promised to have our new indoor bathroom finished, something I've wanted for years. Please come. We would love to see you.

Thank you for being such a good friend. I could never have gotten through my months in Sioux Falls without you.

Love, Gretchen'

"Isn't that nice, Billy? She doesn't know that we have already made up, but I'll write and tell her. I really have missed her. She is a little older than me and sort of quiet, but she was always pleasant, never said a word against anyone. Maybe I should try to be more like her in that respect, do you think?" she said wryly, looking impishly at Billy, her brown eyes twinkling.

He sat beside her and said, "Don't you ever change one thing." He kissed her again and put his arm around her on the back of the swing. They rocked slowly for a few minutes, taking care not to make too much noise. Then he asked, "What was it you wanted to talk to me about, sweetheart?"

"Well honey, I've been thinking."

"Oh oh"

"Come on now. Be serious. We've been going together and working together for a few years now and I think we know where we' re headed – at least everybody else does – and since I got Gretchen's letter wondered why we keep on waiting. We have quite a bit of money saved up. We don't need to put off a decision any longer, do we?"

**148**

Her eyes were large with hopeful desire, totally melting any resistance Billy might have had. He enveloped her in his strong arms and kissed her with passion. The swing ceased its squeaking.

She pulled away, quite breathless, and he said earnestly, "I love you so much Louisa. Please marry me, the sooner the better."

Her eyes sparkled, but she said solemnly, "Yes, Billy honey, yes, but you know that will mean that I'll have to quit my job. Mr. Simpson would never stand for both of us to be working at the hotel once we are married."

"Of course you'll quit," he said firmly. "No wife of mine is going to work if I can help it. You'll keep our house and take care of the kids, and I'll go to work just like all the other happily married couples."

She giggled, "Except for those out-of-state divorcees."

"Yeah, well, that's different."

So it was settled. They set a date to be married in November at the St. Olaf Lutheran Church, and happily endured the teasing of their friends when they announced their plans the next evening in the hotel kitchen. The sisters now had another room to fill, but had ceased to worry about it, since every vacancy had been filled almost immediately.

Their perennial guests, Abner Faraday and Ignacious Wiggins, became permanent fixtures, paying for their room and board with regularity and regarding the boarding house as their home and the roomers who came and went as their transitional family. Eventually, as the years brought changes, the house would contain only the sisters and the two gentlemen, who aged and died, leaving only Mina, who would sell the house for a tidy sum and move into one of the nice apartments at the Brown Apartment House across from the post office, where she would live out her life amid her memorabilia.

One blustery November day Hank and Mike were stopped on their way to work by Shorty who was stationed at his spot in front of the Cataract Hotel. He was sticking out the weather until it turned too cold even for him.

"Whadya want, Shorty?" asked Mike. He drew his jacket closer around him and stayed where he was, not moving toward him. He had learned his lesson and tried to steer clear of the dirty little man, pathetic though he was.

"Don't git yer dander up, boy. I need a favor done, that's

all. Won't take but a minute and I'll pay ya."

The bellhops shifted from one foot to the other in the brisk wind, and listened at a distance.

"Ya remember that Bart Kelly fella?"

They nodded. "What about him?"

"Well, he's in jail and he needs some things."

It was common knowledge that Shorty spent part of his day visiting the jail, talking to the prisoners through the low windows. He made a few dollars doing errands for them.

The hops looked at each other, wondering what Bart Kelly had done to merit being put in jail. The county jail was a most unsavory place to be, even for the worst kind of criminal. It stood directly north of the Minnehaha County Courthouse. A wooden structure, it was connected to the Courthouse by a narrow boardwalk. It was in poor condition and was inadequate for the use made of it. It was, in general, a fire hazard and in such deplorable condition that law abiding citizens were up in arms about it, demanding that a new, decent place of incarceration be built.

"What'd he do for Pete's sake?" asked Hank.

"Wal, ya know how he sells corsets and fits them on all those lonely divorsays in there?" and he gave a wicked wink as he jerked his head to the hotel behind him. "He finally got caught taking liberties with one of them, Leastways tha's what she claims. Old Bart said he had a female in attendance for propriety's sake, but turns out she warn't no lady, if ya git my drift." His nasty laugh made the hops squirm and they moved away from him.

"Now just a durned minute. Old Bart just needs some stuff from Olson's Drug Store. Appears he caught cold in that jail. He gave me money for some of that honey syrup and Perry Davis's Pain Killer, a bottle of each. Said he's shakin' all over with the ague from the dampness in that place and needs medicine fast. Here, see? Here's the two bucks and two more for your trouble. Won't take you but a few minutes to fetch it to me."

"What's in it for you?" asked Mike, suspicious.

"Why, ain't nothin'' nothin' at all. Can't a fella do a good deed now'n then?"

His toothless grin was not convincing, but the hops looked at one another and decided to do it. After all, it wouldn't take long and to be sick in that awful jail was like a sentence of death.

Hank was curious. "What kind of liberties did he take?"

"Don't know fer sure, but I kin imagine. Fittin' them corsets on them pretty ladies has to be a pleasant occupation, don't ya think? But he was charged with bein' a con man and a insult to God."

"Criminy," shivered Mike.

"Git goin' now and bring me that there medicine, and I'll take it to old Bart straight away."

The hops took off on a run. Shorty took a swig from his bottle. The liquid seemed to warm him as it slid down his throat and dribbled from his unsightly chin whiskers. He chuckled to himself as he thought what the prohibitionists had said when he had been cornered one day and forced to listen to a lecture on the evils of "liquid fire." He took another swallow and smiled at an oncoming customer who needed a shine.

The medicine was duly delivered to Bart Kelly by Shorty, who actually had done a good deed, with no one to know of it except for Bart, who paid him several dollars for his efforts on his behalf. In the telling of Shorty's good deed he was not believed, and Shorty had to settle for the warm feeling his deed gave him for the short time it lasted. With the money he received from Bart he had given a dollar to each of the hops and with the rest he bought a bottle of liquor.

When Bart Kelly was taken to court coughing and close to pneumonia he was represented by Jonathan Williams of the firm of Grafton and Willians, whose impassioned plea moved the judge to be lenient, considering the condition of the defendant and the frivolous charge made against him. He was levied a fine which he easily paid, returned to the Cataract where he quickly packed his bags and checked out without bidding farewell to any of the lovelies whose company he had enjoyed for months. He boarded the Illinois Central at once for sunnier climes.

The Sioux Falls Savings Bank in the southeast corner of the lobby of the Cataract Hotel was a very profitable institution, not only for the citizenry, but also as the repository for the money of the various guests of the hotel, proving to be a distinct convenience for ease in depositing and withdrawing sums without leaving the building.

On a chilly, but bright sunny day in November, Clare Clayborne emerged from the elevator and crossed the lobby in determined steps, her back straight, her head held high, staring straight ahead. Through the windows of the bank she was seen approaching and the door was opened by a courteous gentleman as she continued her stride, unabated, and walked through the doorway without so much as a thank you or acknowledgement. However, no offense was taken, because by now most establishments were accustomed to the ways and snobish conduct of Mrs. Clare Clayborne. All of them had benefitted from the ways she spent her money.

She walked directly to the desk of an important looking man seated in the far corner. He smiled amiably at her as she sat down and got down to business. She withdrew a sum of money and requested a bank draft for $3,000 to be made out to Alphonse Grafton, Attorney at Law. The man complied with her wishes without question, not even raising an eyebrow. One of the bank's strong points was complete privacy for its customers and discretion on the part of its employees. Time had come for the lady's divorce and for her to pay the piper were the banker's thoughts, but he merely handed over the money cordially. She accepted the bills and the bank draft and tucked them into her fancy beaded purse. She lifted her head resolutely, rose and said she would be returning soon to close out her account and for the bank to have all figures ready for her. She took no notice of him as the banker rose and smiled and said he was happy to serve her. She turned and walked away, ignoring the man who stood at the door with the door open as she swept out. All eyes were upon the elegant woman as she moved toward the elevator, and they knew her feelings were not as unfeeling as she would like them to believe.

When she got to her room and closed the door, she leaned against it and caught her breath, and the sadness threatened to overwhelm her. A maid appeared and she drew herself together and told her that she would be in her bedroom for awhile and did not wish to be disturbed.

She closed the bedroom door and sat at the desk. She drew a diary from a drawer, took a key from her purse and unlocked it, and leafed through its pages filled with her bold handwriting, reading a few words here and there, She turned it to one of the last few pages and began to write:

"Tomorrow I go to court. How I dread it. In vain have I waited for Edmund to come for me or to at least write and tell me he is sorry, that he loves me and wants me back. Have I made a grievous mistake? Have I acted too rashly? Edmund, dear sweet Edmund, I miss you so. I love only you. And the children – what have I done?"

She bowed her head as tears dropped on the page, smudging her words. She buried her head in her arms on the desk and sobbed uncontrollably in despair.

# CHAPTER SEVENTEEN

# *The Divorce*

The Minnehaha County Courthouse was comparatively new, having been designed by Dakota territorial architect, Wallace L. Dow, in 1888-1889. It was a massive building with an exterior of pink Sioux quartzite and was located on the corner of 6th Street and Main Avenue.

Mr. Dow was rightfully proud of the structure and boasted it to be the largest courthouse between Chicago and Denver. A 150 foot high clock tower rose above the east entrance and could be seen for blocks, dominating the landscape. The main entrance was on the east and two tiers of granite steps led up to it. Rimming the steps on each side were curved trims of pink granite leading to double doors with windows of equal size on either side. Arched windows rose above the doors. The south entrance was almost as impressive. On all sides of the building were tall windows topped with decorative stained glass inserts.

The floors of the entryways were laid with large black and white marble tiles and the areas were lighted by large metal chandeliers, which had electric lamps covered by decorated glass shades with scalloped edges emanating from them. Similar chandeliers, painted gold, hung from the high ceilings throughout the building. On the other side of each entryway were heavy circular brass coat racks. The lower part of the inner walls were lined with oak wainscoting, and set at intervals against the walls were gold painted iron radiators with flat mottled tops which heated the cavernous building in the winter, oftentimes hissing with escaping steam.

Wide panels of fancy scrolled oak trim decorated the windows and doors. The floors shone with polished hardwood. A visitor's eyes were drawn to a dramatic stairway a short distance from the entrances. The steps were wide and deep, made of iron and slate, and bordered by a railing supported by fancy black iron grillwork. The stairs and landing were bright from a skylight high above. At the top of the stairway was an archway decorated with a delicate gold ornamental trim.

The large courtroom on the second floor was roomy, lined with tall windows which let in air and light beautifully through the stained glass inserts. The biggest and fanciest gold colored chandelier in the entire place hung from high in the center of the ceiling, circled with numerous scalloped glass shades covering the electric lamps. Immediately above the grand fixture was a round metal grill of elaborate design of the same size. The perforations in the grill permitted the free flow of air which cooled the courtroom in the summer. Small brass light fixtures dotted the walls of the courtroom. Directly opposite the entrance to the room and some distance on the west end was a raised platform where the judge sat behind a high dais. There was a witness dock on each side. Seats for a jury were on the south wall behind a wood enclosure. A short distance from the entrance, looking toward the judge's platform, were rows of wood spectator seats encased in black iron grillwork. The hard seats were on hinges and each had a wire receptacle for a gentleman's hat fastened to the bottom.

The whole effect of the magnificent courthouse was one of the dignified administration of justice, imparting a subdued atmosphere to those who entered its confines.

It was the middle of November, 1904, and the fall season was in full swing with balls at the Cataract Hotel and Chataqua presentations of recitals and plays held in the 3,000 seat auditorium on the second floor of City Hall. Indoor activities took the place of the diversions of the Big Sioux River which was now covered with a thin film of ice, not yet firm enough for skating.

Clare Clayborne had only one communication with her lawyer, the infamous Alphonse Grafton, since her encounter with Dehlia Van Tassel, who was long gone, but who had left her mark on the City of Sioux Falls. Clare had refused to take his calls over the telephone or in person when a maid would present her with his calling card, except for the first one, when she determined the time of her divorce hearing, what was expected of her, and the amount of his fee. He had quoted the sum of $3,000 and she did not argue, although she felt she was paying for a professional escort in view of all that had transpired since her arrival in the city in April on a pleasant afternoon. It all seemed so long ago. It was hard to recall the previous steamy summer as a cold wind howled outside her hotel window. She prayed it would not snow before she could leave South Dakota for Chicago and home.

Home, how foreign the word sounded to her. Her home would be the residence she had shared with Edmund for so many years, and her children would be with her. However, Edmund would not be. Her worst fears had been realized when he made no effort to get in touch with her; he had not beseeched her to come back to him. She had been so sure that he would. She might have swallowed her pride and gone back to him. But how could she at this point? Things had gone too far to turn back. And she was still hurt by his casting her aside for another woman, a far younger woman. The thought had crossed her mind that perhaps she had not been the only one. She didn't understand it at all. Her pride and honor simply could not accept what he had done to her. She would obtain her divorce.

She looked at her reflection in the mirror above her dresser. She was still striking, a lovely woman with perfect skin and deep blue eyes. Her hair was sleek and shining. She had a good figure. Why couldn't Edmund love her as she had loved him, as she still loved him. Why had he preferred other women? She sighed deeply and stifled a sob. She would simply have to forget him, as hard as that might be. She would just not think about him anymore. The problem would soon be resolved. She would get her divorce with the assistance of that disgusting Alphonse Grafton, pay him his fee and leave as soon as possible. She would start a new life in her own home with her two children. Her mother could move in and they would raise the children together. It would be all right. In spite of her rationale tears filled her eyes. She couldn't let her maids see her in such a state. She stood tall and resolute and began to lay out the clothes she would wear the next day when she would have in her hands the piece of paper, so easily obtained, that would change her life forever.

The sounds of the gaiety of the ball the previous night was succeeded by the sounds of church bells from the St. Olaf Lutheran Church in mid-morning when Billy and Louisa were married amid family and friends, who wished them well. Clare Clayborne could scarcely imagine how there could be so much happiness and laughter when she was so desperately unhappy.

She hadn't slept well, but just before dawn came a few hours of fitful sleep. Her maids had been instructed to pack everything the night before, to take their breakfast in the dining room at their leisure, and to rouse her if she had not awakened by 10:00 o' clock. This unaccustomed liberty could not be enjoyed to the fullest by the young women who had waited on and attended to every whim of the picky Clare Clayborne for months. So they had their breakfast early, ate hurriedly, and returned to the fifth floor suite to await their mistress's awakening and her orders for the day.

All bags and trunks were packed and ready to go, except for a few last minute items. The train tickets had been purchased and lay on the dresser in her bedroom. The hops were to come promptly at 3:30 o'clock to load the luggage into the carriage that was to be ready at the east entrance to the hotel to take them to the Milwaukee Depot the short distance to 5th Street and Phillips Avenue. They would use the sleeping car and arrive in Chicago the next morning. The maids hoped they could all sleep without interruption and get some rest on their way to Chicago where they had been employed months before, with no disturbing incident. They had been hired for temporary service to assist Mrs. Clayborne during her South Dakota residency. It had proved to be an experience they would never forget and, in the event they were not hired for extended employment, they felt certain they would get good recommendations, considering the extreme conditions of their present employment.

They sat quietly in the sitting room of the suite and waited, commenting on the bells pealing from the direction of the church and envying Billy and Louisa, with whom they had become somewhat acquainted during their stay. What a nice couple they were and how they longed for such a bright future some day.

They didn't have to wait very long for a summons from Mrs. Clayborne. She emerged from her bedroom, somewhat disheveled with swollen eyes and uncombed hair, and expressed a desire for a warm bath and help in getting dressed. She looked tired and wan, pale from lack of any real rest. Her ordeal was coming to an end and she was resigned to her fate. The faint lines around her lovely mouth were plainly visible and for a few minutes they felt sorry for their demanding mistress.

Clare bathed and relaxed in the warm, soapy water and

was somewhat rejuvenated when she stepped from the tub into the warm towel her maids held for her. They powdered her and dressed her, all except for her velvet dress and the new dark blue hat with the plum colored plume. They fastened a pale violet colored velvet ribbon around her slim neck which held a cameo at the throat. Then she put on a frilly robe and ordered them to call for a bite of breakfast and a pot of coffee, which they scurried to do. She had been courteous and polite to them, throwing them off balance. Clare sat dejected in the small sitting room, her chin cupped in her hand, looking out the window at the sunny sky filled with puffy white clouds being pushed across the cold sky by the unrelenting wind.

She was still sitting thus when they returned. They paused, hesitating to disturb her, but she stirred, waved them in, and let them arrange her napkin on her lap and pour her a cup of the steaming coffee. Then she dismissed them, admonishing them to be ready to leave upon her return from the courthouse, as she wished to absent herself from the City of Sioux Falls and the wild State of South Dakota as soon as possible.

At the appointed time of 1:30 o'clock Clare Clayborne emerged from the elevator, to all appearances no different from her presence on previous occasions, and walked with purpose to the east entrance of the lobby. She passed the Sioux Falls Savings Bank, ignoring the nod of the man who only that morning had handed over to her the remaining funds she had left in the bank. Alphonse Grafton was waiting for her at the entrance, having been forbidden to come up to the suite to escort her down.

"Good afternoon, my dear Clare. May I say—"

She did not speak to him, only glared at him with enough spite in her eyes to stop the flattery beginning to drip from his lips beneath his curled mustache. He cleared his throat and opened the door as she walked through without breaking her stride. She permitted him to assist her into the carriage, but totally ignored him on the brief ride.

The carriage stopped at the east entrance to the courthouse and Mr. Grafton took her gloved hand to assist her descent. She stepped to the sidewalk and stopped for a moment to take in the impressive edifice before her. White clouds were scudding across the sky in the bright afternoon sunshine, seeming to move just above the tall clock tower, making her slightly light headed. Mr. Grafton took her elbow lest she fall but, regaining her balance, she ascended the granite steps, refusing further assistance. He opened one of the heavy doors and she stepped inside onto the marble tiles and through the entryway into the interior of the building. The radiators gave off a faint warm glow, just enough to take the chill off the November afternoon.

She walked toward the stairway with its wide slate steps set in the middle of the room and looked up, with her hand on the black railing. The area was very bright with sunlight coming through the lofty skylight. She began to climb and paused on the landing to look upward once more, gazing at the cloud filled sky bright with sunlight streaming through the skylight. The cheery atmosphere was charming, but it did not lift her dark mood and she could not sustain the warm feeling of the area. She turned and continued to the top through the prettily decorated archway. She glanced at Mr. Grafton and he motioned in the direction of the doorway to the courtroom and opened it with a grand gesture and a bow. She walked through stiffly and looked straight ahead.

Judge Addison had just entered and taken his seat on the platform behind the dais and watched in appreciation as the elegant woman approached in a dignified manner through the aisle between the spectator seats. His clerk sat at a table in front of him and both of them looked approvingly at the woman walking toward them with Alphonse Grafton in groveling attendance a step behind. This time the lawyer did not appear to be as smug as usual as he guided his client to her freedom and added to his own burgeoning back account.

"Good afternoon, Attorney Grafton. This is your client, Mrs. Clare Clayborne?"

"Yes, your honor," said Mr. Grafton with his usual obsequious manner.

"Please step into the dock, my dear," said Judge Addison kindly, motioning to his left. She stepped up into the circular enclosure and sat down gracefully, looking out at the expansive room. She noted the spectator seats were empty and breathed easier. She gave no hint of her nervousness and fear, fear that her life and all that she had aspired to was slipping away and that she would soon be irretrievably damaged, never to be the same again. And Edmund would never know how she had suffered because of his actions. How unfair life was.

"What are the grounds?, asked the judge as a formality.

"Irreconcilable differences due to the reprehensible conduct of the defendant, Edmund Clayborne, and his dalliance with the young personal maid of the plaintiff, Clare Clayborne, which conduct was adultery, pure and simple, combined with cruel and inhuman treatment and willful neglect, while the plaintiff's conduct was pure and unsullied," replied Mr. Grafton, and he was off into his familiar recital which the judge and his clerk recited silently with him. Mrs. Clayborne folded her gloved hands and waited for him to stop. It all sounded so cheap and tawdry. At least she had avoided the notoriety and publicity her action for divorce would have created in Chicago where they were well known. It would soon be over. She sighed again, then heard Judge Addison say, "Are the allegations as contained in your complaint accurate, Mrs. Clayborne?"

Her mouth was dry as a desert. She swallowed and replied faintly, "Yes."

"Is there no possibility for a reconciliation?"

"None."

"Is there anything you wish to add, my dear?" he asked kindly.

"No, nothing."

"Very well. Custody of the children awarded to the plaintiff, Clare Clayborne. Divorce granted."

Her heart thumped and the lump in her throat grew larger and she was sure her cameo would choke her from the strain of keeping her composure. I will not cry. I mustn't. She took a shuddering breath and looked at Alphonse Grafton whose smug expression infuriated her. The lump disappeared and she was consumed with anger.

"It's over, my dear Clare. You may step down now," he said, smiling at her, mentally calculating the addition to his finances.

She took his hand as he helped her down from the dock. "We shall retire to my office to conclude the matter," he said in a conciliatory manner.

She said nothing but accompanied him, sweeping through the door which he held open for her. Judge Addision and his clerk watched the departure with as much appreciation as they had the grand entrance.

"I'm not so sure about this one," said the judge and his clerk nodded in agreement. "I have a feeling that old Grafton is about to get more than his fee." Then, with a sigh, "Give me a few minutes before the next one. I swear, these divorces are beginning to wear on me." He would surely have to retire soon and write those memoirs.

Clare and her lawyer emerged from the courthouse into the cold afternoon. The sun had disappeared, leaving the wind still chasing the clouds in a darkening sky. She was quiet on the ride to the offices of Grafton and Williams. Mr. Grafton interpreted her silence as acceptance of her situation and of her forgiveness of him for whatever transgression she imagined he might have been guilty of. He had not understood her refusal to see him during the last weeks. He was positive he could have straightened out any misunderstanding there might have been. They had gotten along so well, just as he had gotten on with some of his most attractive clients in the past. Oh well, they would soon part and in the parting they would have their memories and his were of a very pleasant nature, proving once more what an excellent lawyer he was and what a marvelous success with women he maintained. Clare Clayborne would have her freedom which he so skillfully obtained for her, and he would have a fat fee for doing so.

The carriage crossed 9th Street south from the Cataract Hotel and stopped in front of the Edmison-Jameson Building. He helped her down and opened the door to the building for her and led her to the elevator. They didn't speak as they ascended to the fifth floor. Mr. Grafton's fingers followed the curve of his mustache as he smiled, deep in thought. The elevator stopped and he gestured for her to precede him to the door of his office which he opened with flair and authority. She entered with haughty decorum.

"Good afternoon, Mr. Grafton, Mrs. Clayborne," smiled the secretary.

She walked past the young woman with no change in her stride as Mr. Grafton opened his office door and she entered as he made a deep bow. He motioned in the direction of the chair situated before his desk and walked swiftly to his ornate desk and sat down with an air of immense satisfaction. Another job well done, and a most enjoyable one at that. He beamed at her.

"Now then, you are a free woman, Clare. I hope my services have been quite satisfactory."

She spoke her first words to him. "I have your bank draft in the amount of $3,000, Mr. Grafton, which is the sum agreed upon for services rendered in obtaining my divorce."

She placed it carefully before him. He ascertained it to be in order and commenced his closing remarks, but he was a bit offended to find there was no heartfelt thank you from his wealthy client. He raised his eyes to find her looking at him coldly, looking almost through him, her blue eyes like ice. He started to squirm, but began his speech.

"My dear Clare, may I say that you have been, by far, my most distinguished client, one of the most elegant women it has ever been my good fortune to serve, the most—"

"Oh shut up!" she said, raising her voice.

He ceased abruptly, stunned at the outburst, She stood up with her back held stiffly erect, her proud head high, her eyes shooting cold fire at him. She grasped her velvet draw string purse,which exactly matched her hat, in one hand and pointed a gloved finger at him with the other. She could hardly speak she was so consumed with rage, coupled with a sorrow that she could not squelch and for which she held him partly responsible.

"You despicable, pompous bore," she spat at him in a voice that was steadily losing control.

"My dear Clare, I don't understand—" he sputtered as he started to get up from his massive chair.

"Sit down!" she said with authority. He did as she commanded. "Now you listen." She moved closer to the desk, leaned over slightly with her finger pointing dangerously close to his nose, causing his mustache to quiver, and said unflinchingly,

"You obtained a divorce for me which I asked for and for which I have paid you. But you betrayed me. In my desperately unhappy state you came to my rescue. You wined and dined me, flattered me, and led me to believe that I was important to you. You comforted me when I needed comfort and I thought you were sincere. I realized only too late that this is all standard procedure for you, something you do by rote, and I foolishly proved to be as gullible as the rest of your women clients. You have made me grievously ashamed of myself and of my conduct with you. And I can assure you, Alphonse Grafton, I am not accustomed to being shamed!"

"But, Clare—"

He pressed back into his chair as she leaned closer with her pointing finger, her eyes flashing.

"You took advantage of me, of my vulnerable state. I shared

my innermost thoughts with you and you took my confidence and betrayed it. You took me to supper, you took me to entertainments in an effort to take my mind off my suffering and to cloud my mind as to what you were doing."

She paused and clutched her heaving bosom. Her cheeks flamed from her emotional outburst. As she went on with her tirade venom fairly dripped as she said, "And you took me to bed!" She shouted out the words in her disgust. "You sullied my good reputation and then you took my money, you loathsome bastard!"

Her voice surely must have reached the waiting room. Mr. Grafton sank further into his chair. He didn't know how to cope with the situation, which was an entirely new one to him. He was no longer in charge. Most of his other clients had been most grateful for his attentions.

She stood back from the desk and regained some of her composure, but she was shaking from her outburst and from the release of her former suppression of a rage that had consumed her. She lowered her voice.

"Tell me, Alphie," and she accentuated the name, at which Alphonse Grafton groaned and covered his eyes. "Why do you do it? Why do you court married women you cannot possibly have – you, a married man who regularly commits adultery. Why? Is it the thrill of conquest? Is that uppermost in your little mind simply because you are in a position to accomplish it? You misuse your power and authority. You prey on women. You are a nasty, wicked man."

Her eyes were a smoldering blue fire. He could no longer look at her. She gathered herself together, composed her expression, and turned to leave. As she grasped the doorknob she turned to glare at him one last time.

"You really should grow up – Alphie."

With that she opened the door and flung it against the wall where it connected with a bang and, as she swept across the waiting room to the outer door, she was dimly aware of a fat woman sitting in a chair against the wall. As she left the office, leaving the door wide open, she heard,

"Good-bye, Mrs. Clayborne. You can go in now, Mrs. Grafton."

The fat woman heaved herself from the chair, stood with a grim look on her face, and marched into the office where, through the open door was visible the crumpled, despairing figure of her husband.

Clare Clayborne and her two maids left that afternoon on the sleeper train to Chicago. Exhilarated by her unaccustomed expression of outrage she ordered champagne before supper for all of them. Then she asked the young women to continue in her employment if they would be so kind, thereby taking the first step in putting their adventure in Sioux Falls, South Dakota, behind them.

Later that week, at the Cataract Hotel, the last of the guests departed in a flurry of November wind and dust. Billy gave a sigh of relief. It had been quite a season, with more to come, but the winter had to be less hectic. He barely caught his breath when a horse drawn omnibus careened around the corner with an unfamiliar man in the driver's seat. He was shouting and roaring with laughter as he pulled in the reins on the horses that had just enjoyed an unaccustomed spirited gallop from the Illinois Central Depot. They came to a halt too far up 9th Street hill and had to be coaxed backwards to the entrance, much against their wills. Consequently, the travelers had to alight from the crowded vehicle a few feet past their desired stopping point. Besides the driver there were five occupants, plus two female servants who clung to the sides at the rear where mounds of luggage were stacked. The servants had terrified looks on their faces, which were made rosy from the cold and the wind, and the others were yelling their approval at the diversion from their long trip. The horses snorted and pawed the pavement.

The first to emerge was a somewhat disheveled, but flashily dressed woman with a cigarette holder in her hand. She was followed by a female companion who was laughing loudly, two men who shouted encouragement to their driver, the two female servants, and the regular driver who stepped down last with a sheepish expression on his flushed face. He quickly took the reins from the man who was loudly chastising the horses for not backing up, and accepted a number of bills for his trouble, whereupon his face was wreathed with smiles and he thanked the man profusely.

"Thank you, my good sir. That was invigorating," said the man as he released the reins and flung his cape over a shoulder flamboyantly.

Billy summoned his bellhops to renewed service. They walked up the sidewalk and gathered up the numerous items of luggage, hat boxes and packages, and returned to the hotel. Billy stood at his station and opened the doors wide for the loud procession as they entered, disturbing Mr. Simpson who was arranging the keys in their cubbyholes for his new guests. The woman with the cigarette holder gave Billy a flirtatious smile and proceeded to the registration desk. Mr. Simpson turned, curved his crimson mouth into a haughty smile, and wearily considered the noisy people before the desk and the man with the cape and windblown hair under a strange looking hat with a wide brim.

"Mr. Gilmore, I presume? We were expecting you some time ago with the others."

"We took a little joy ride, you might say. Loads of fun. In answer to your question, yes, that's me, Paul Gilmore, actor. I'm sure you've heard of me." He said it more as a statement of fact than an inquiry and did not look up as he signed his name with broad strokes, not expecting an answer. "This is my wife, Dolly – Dolly Madison. I'm sure you've heard of her."

"Ah yes," replied Mr. Simpson with feigned affirmation. "You have several rooms, Mr. Gilmore? Might I have made an error in this assumption?"

"No error, you are absolutely right. I need lots of rooms for all my friends – and my wife – until she and I can find a house that is suitable to wait out the winter. She'll have her house and I'll have mine. You do have lodgings in this town, do you not? She and I shall get along much better apart in our own separate houses until we get our – problems resolved. Isn't that right, my sweet?"

Dolly Madison Gilmore puffed lazily on a cigarette in the long holder, paying no attention to him, and sending puffs of smoke in his direction.

Mr. Simpson was shocked.

Mrs. Goldworthy was writing furiously in her tablet. Just wait until the Bishop hears about this.

### THE END

# ACKNOWLEDGEMENTS

*A Comprehensive History of Minnehaha County, South Dakota,* by Charles A. Smith, 1949.

*An Economic and Social Survey of Sioux Falls, South Dakota, 1938-39,* by Arthur G. Horton, 1939.

Florence Ditmanson.

*Letters from a Dakota Divorcee'* by Jane Burr, 1907.

Bob Kolbe.

Acie W. Matthews.

*Minnehaha County Historical and Biographical Sketches,* Minnehaha County Historical Society, 1987.

*Sioux Falls in Retrospect* by R. E. Bragstad, 1967.

*Sioux Falls, South Dakota,* a Pictorial History, by Gary D. Olson and Erik L. Olson, 1985.

Siouxland Heritage Museums, with special thanks to Bill Hoskins.

*The South Dakota Challenge* by Robert F. Karolevitz, 1975.

*South Dakota History, Money Versus Morality: The Divorce Industry of Sioux Falls,* by Connie DeVelder Schaffer.

South Dakota State Historical Society.

Leonard Tripp.

*Uniquely South Dakota* by Bob Karolevitz and Bernie Hunhoff, 1988.

University of South Dakota Law Library.

*Where the Sioux River Bends, a Newspaper Chronicle,* by Wayne Fanebust, 1985.

# POSTSCRIPT

I want to assure my readers that this is a fictional account of what might have happened to the characters depicted in the story during their six to seven months stay in the State of South Dakota, and specifically the City of Sioux Falls, as they waited out their residency to obtain their divorces.

The references to the Bishop are in no way meant to detract from the admirable efforts of Bishop William Hobart Hare of the Calvary Episcopal Church, who was instrumental in eventually getting the residency law changed to a full year in 1908. He further succeeded in changing the court appearances for divorcees from closed court to open court for any spectators who wished to observe the proceedings.

Lawyers were chagrined.